BUTLER THE TOURIST

"You are a spy!" the man shouted at Butler in a thick Russian accent.

"Who me?" Butler asked. *"I'm just an American tourist."*

"Sit down!" the Russian said, pointing to a chair with shackles. *"Now—permit me to introduce myself. I am Major Alexei Ospenko of the People's Secret Police, better known to you perhaps as the KGB."*

"Howdy," Butler said irreverently. *"And my name's Butler. I'd like to speak to someone at the United States Embassy, if you don't mind."*

"We do mind," Ospenko said quietly. *"You will speak to us only. What are you doing in the Soviet Union?"*

"Sightseeing mostly. You know—St. Basil's Cathedral, Lenin's Tomb, the Kremlin. All the hot spots."

"Have you seen Kaluga Prison yet?" Ospenko asked him. *"But then again, you couldn't have, because no one ever returns from there..."*

BUTLER

SMART BOMBS

Philip Kirk

LEISURE BOOKS • NEW YORK CITY

In the councils of government, we must guard against the acquisition of unwarranted influence, whether sought or unsought, by the military-industrial complex. The potential for the disastrous rise of misplaced power exists and will persist. We must never let the weight of the combination endanger our liberties or democratic process.

Dwight D. Eisenhower
January 17, 1961

A LEISURE BOOK

Published by

Nordon Publications, Inc.
Two Park Avenue
New York, N.Y. 10016

1

A submarine surfaced through the black water of the Baltic Sea. It was a foggy night in November and a breeze whistled through the antennae of the submarine's conning tower. Hatches were opened in the conning tower, foredeck, and afterdeck. Men in black suits poured out of the hatches and took positions at the guns on deck. One group of men pulled a black rubber boat across the glistening wet deck.

Behind the boat walked Butler, a tall broad-shouldered man in a black turtleneck sweater and black stockingcap on his head. He carried a Colt .45 in a shoulder holster and an old British commando knife on his belt. His face was covered with black camouflage paint. He watched grimly as the crew lowered the rubber boat over the sides.

"Good luck, Butler," said Captain Sinclair.

"Thanks." Butler turned and a sailor handed him the rope. Butler held onto it with both hands and went over the side of the submarine, like a mountain climber descending. He let go of the rope when his feet hit the rubber boat, then he quickly cast away the other lines. Kneeling in the boat, he grasped the oars and pushed himself toward shore.

He could hear sailors running along the deck of the submarine, and then he heard the hatches being closed. The submarine glided away from him, and he turned in time to see it angle into the sea. It disappeared quickly, and Butler was alone on the Baltic.

He looked at his watch; it was one o'clock in the morning. The shore was due south and he checked his compass to make certain he was headed in that direction. He pushed the oars with firm, strong strokes, hoping that nothing would go wrong.

He was headed for a stretch of shore east of the city of Tallinn, on the Estonia Coast of the USSR. A top Soviet scientist was defecting, and Butler was going to pick him up. The scientist had been furnishing information to Butler's organization for ten years, but now the jaws of the KGB were closing on him and he had to flee. Butler, the ex-CIA troubleshooter, was given the hazardous mission.

Butler's organization was called the Bancroft Research Institute, whose overt purpose was to conduct scientific research for businesses and governments throughout the world, and whose covert function was to maintain peace by doing everything possible to keep the hawks of various countries from going to war against each other.

Butler rowed toward the shore he couldn't see, riding over the huge swells and listening for trouble. The Soviets patrolled their coastlines well, because they didn't want anyone to enter or leave without authorization. A foggy, moonless night had been chosen because of the cover it afforded.

He estimated that he was around five hundred yards from shore. Bringing in the oars, he knelt in the rubber boat and took his Electronic Direction Finder (EDF) from its rubber case. He clicked the switch on and was about to press the button when he heard the faint rumble of a motor craft.

Clutching the EDF to his belly, he dived to the bottom of the rubber boat and lay motionless. The sound of the motor grew louder; it was doubtless a Soviet patrol craft. These waters were said to be swarming with them, and Butler had been warned that he could expect to encounter at least one.

Butler lay in the bottom of the rubber boat that was tossed about by the waves. He, the boat, and everything on it was covered with dull black paint that blended with the night. Even if a searchlight was trained on him, it wouldn't see

6

anything, unless it was very close. Butler hoped that patrol boat wouldn't get too close. The odds were that it wouldn't, but Butler knew from bitter experience that the odds could turn against you in a very ugly way.

The patrol boat motored closer and closer. Butler peeked over the side of the rubber boat and saw a searchlight cutting a golden swath through the fog. His heart froze with the thought that maybe there was a tip-off and they were looking specifically for him. He'd been betrayed before; it wouldn't be anything new. In the spy game you had to expect it.

The searchlight beam headed his way and he ducked, staring coolly into the bottom of the boat. Butler was not one to panic; otherwise he would have been dead long ago. Instead, he thought strategically. If they came for him he'd shoot out the searchlight and hope they couldn't find him again in the tractless, foggy sea. If they did catch him he'd surrender with a smile and say he was a shipwrecked sailor.

The searchlight beam passed over him and kept going; they didn't even see him. He breathed more easily. The patrol boat crossed his bow and then the sound of the motors began to recede. It was on a routine tour of the coastline, and eyes on routine tours are never that sharp.

When the sea was quiet again, Butler raised himself to a kneeling position. He switched on the EDF and pushed the button twice, thus transmitting a signal toward shore. He waited and listened, bouncing on top of the waves, and then he heard three beeps come from his receiver. It was Dr. Kahlovka answering, he hoped. A tiny light flashed on the compass of the EDF, indicating the direction the signal had come from. Butler grabbed the oars again and pushed in the direction indicated by the light.

Now he had something new to worry about. What if Dr. Kahlovka had been captured, tortured, and made to reveal everything? In that case, there might be a patrol of KGB agents on the beach waiting to see who'd show up. If so, there'd be a large number of them and it'd be senseless to try and fight it out. He'd surrender meekly and try to sell his shipwrecked sailor story. Somehow he didn't think they'd buy it, and then the fun would begin. But he'd cross that bridge when he came to it. No use worrying needlessly.

He rowed toward shore, his shoulders not sore at all. He worked out regularly in gymnasiums and could bench-press 260 pounds. And he wasn't winded, because he jogged like everybody else these days. Butler was a magnificent physical specimen for his 32 years, but he knew that nobody was stronger than a bullet.

He peered into the darkness ahead and could make out nothing at all. The fog was thick as the proverbial pea soup, but he must be nearing shore. Shipping his oars again, he bent over the EDF and pressed the button twice. It immediately beeped three times and the light on the compass told him to steer a few degrees to the west.

He continued rowing, and then suddenly he was aware of the sound of surf ahead of him. That meant that the beach was only another fifty yards or so away. He squinted and kept rowing, but still could see nothing. Maneuvering adroitly with his oars, he got on top of a wave and rode it like a surfboard toward shore. The wind whistling in his ears, he smiled as he and his rubber boat soared over the top of the water. It reminded him of the surf at Malibu Beach, where he'd once shared a little house with a certain female who played bit roles in Hollywood movies. Someone else probably was sharing her house right now, while he was about to share a beach with person or persons unknown.

The wave cut away and the rubber boat skidded on top of the wet sand. Butler jumped out agilely and dragged it to shore and up the sandy hill to a spot where the water wouldn't reach it. Now he had to move fast. He took his flashlight from his belt, pointed it straight ahead into the fog, and hit the button once quickly. He waited anxiously, his heart beating in his chest, and several long seconds later he saw a light flash once in the fog. Gritting his teeth, he took out his Colt .45, slipped off the safety, and got ready for the worst.

He heard footsteps running across the sand. Cocking his ear, they sounded like only one pair of feet, and that was good news. A dark figure came to him out of the fog. He pointed his Colt .45 at it. The figure dropped to its knees in front of him, and Butler found himself staring into the face of an attractive young woman.

"They got my father," she said breathlessly.

"Oh." Butler tried to think strategically. The KGB might have got her father, or she might be a KGB agent herself.

"Are you alone?" he asked.

"Of course I'm alone."

"Does anyone know you're here?"

"I don't think so."

"Do you have any weapons with you?"

"A knife."

"Let's get out of here. Help me push the boat into the water."

They got on each side of the boat and dragged it into the crashing waves. When they were up to their knees, Butler told her to get in. She climbed into the rubber boat, and he pushed it out farther until the water was up to his thighs, making his legs numb with cold. Then he climbed into the boat with her.

"Sit over there," he said, pointing to the bow.

She moved to the front of the rubber boat and he kneeled facing her, taking the oars in hand and pushing hard to break out of the surf and into the open sea. They climbed up and down the waves, and he saw her hanging onto the ropes on the gunwales. Finally they were free of the surf, but Butler maintained his steady rowing pace. Her pretty face floated in front of him, filtered through fog and framed by a black kerchief.

"What's your name?" he asked.

"Natalia Kahlovka."

"When did they pick up your father?"

"Sometime yesterday—I don't know for sure. A friend of his at the laboratory called me. I was at the university at the time. I left after my classes and went to the place where he hid this." She held her EDF in the air. "Then I went to the rendezvous spot. I've been waiting for you since sundown."

9

"I'm surprised they didn't pick you up at the same time they picked him up."

"What do you mean by that?"

"You were a loose end. I'm surprised the KGB let you go."

Her voice became angry. "You think maybe I am a spy myself?"

"I don't know who you are, lady, but if you try anything funny I'll kill you."

In the dense fog he could see emotions working on her face; maybe she was trying to keep from crying. If she really was Kahlovka's daughter she must have had a hard day and she didn't need him to harass her, but Butler had learned long ago to expect the worst of any situation.

The chugging sound of a Soviet patrol craft came to his ears.

"Get down!" he said to her.

They ducked into the rubber boat and lay together, bodies touching and faces inches apart. He looked into her eyes; they were green and slanted. Blonde hair showed beneath her kerchief and she had the high cheekbones of a Tartar. They looked at each other impassively, their breath intermingling. The sound of the patrol craft came closer. She bit her lower lip.

"Not a sound," he whispered.

She didn't reply, but her eyes indicated she didn't like him very much. He raised his head and looked over her shoulder at the patrol boat heading straight for them, its searchlight slicing through the fog.

He lowered his head. "It's going to be close. I'd better cover your face."

He put his big blackened hands over her white cheeks so they wouldn't catch the shine of the searchlight. Her skin was soft and smooth, and her eyes were like those of a frightened rabbit. There still was white showing, so he covered her face with his, cheeks touching, and the patrol boat rumbled closer. It sounded as though it might ram them. He felt her stiffen against him. Her hands grasped his biceps, but he removed them gently and put them against his chest where they wouldn't show. Then he covered her face with his hands again.

"Don't move," he said.

A sob escaped from her lips.

"Ssshhh."

They lay together, touching as the patrol boat bore down on them. Butler felt her cheeks, torso, and knees against him. He thought it curious that he was having an erotic reaction to the desperate situation. Snuggling closer to her, he kissed her cheek and she took a deep breath. She turned her lips to him and they kissed as the patrol boat closed in on them. The black rubber boat bobbed over the waves, and the girl's body strained against Butler as they tried to hide in each other.

The patrol boat moved away from them. They separated and Butler looked over his shoulder at the patrol boat chugging down the coast, its searchlight splaying over the Baltic Sea.

Butler got to his knees and took the oars in his hands again. Natalia sat in the bow of the boat facing him, studying his face, her hands touching between her knees.

"What is your name?" she asked.

"Butler."

"Is that your first name or your last name?"

"Last name."

"What is your first name?"

"I don't like my first name, so I never use it."

"That's silly."

"Not to me."

"Do you still think I'm some sort of counterspy?"

"It's a possibility. It's also a possibility that I'm a KGB agent on a mission to find out what you know."

"I doubt that."

"You shouldn't doubt anything. This is a very tricky world."

Her face became sad and she closed her eyes. "I wonder what they're doing to father."

"Don't think about it. It can't help him and can only hurt you."

11

Butler's strong arms pushed the oars again and again. The rubber boat moved farther into the Baltic Sea. He checked his compass to make certain he was going in the correct direction. He wanted to head north toward the general direction of Finland, which was the safest direction to go.

"We're awfully far from shore," she said.

"Let's hope so."

"I hope the boat doesn't sink."

"Don't worry about it."

"But I can't swim, you see."

"The boat's not going to sink."

"My father gave me very important information to pass along to your superiors."

"What is it?"

"It is written on papers that I have here." She tapped her breast.

"Can't you tell me?"

"It's very scientific and I don't understand it myself. It has to do with laser beams."

"How come you don't understand it? Aren't you a scientist too?"

"Oh, no. I'm not scientific at all. I study English and French Literature at the University of Leningrad. Or I did until yesterday."

"It's about laser beams, you say?"

"Laser beams and smart bombs."

"It must have something to do with new weapons. The new generation of smart bombs is guided by laser beams."

"I do not know about those things, I'm afraid. If you ask me about Dostoyevsky's tragic sense of life I could tell you all about it, but not laser beams and intelligent bombs. Why are they intelligent?"

"Because they almost never miss. They're guided to their targets by laser beams aimed by soldiers. As long as the soldier can keep his target in his sights, the smart bomb will hit it. A smart bomb costing one thousand dollars can demolish a tank costing a million and a half dollars, and do it easily."

Natalia raised her hand to her mouth. "I think I'm getting ill."

"Seasickness?"

"I think so."

"I have some dramamine pills here." Butler let go of the oars, reached under his turtleneck sweater, and took out a little black tin box. He opened it and picked out two little pills, which he handed to her. "Take these."

"You have some water?"

He reached into a compartment on the inside wall of the rubber boat and took out a black canteen, which he handed to her. She popped the pills into her mouth, took a drink of water, and handed him the canteen back. He returned it to the compartment and took up the oars again.

"Where are we going?" she asked.

"You'll see soon enough."

"Surely you're not going to row all the way to Finland."

"Surely not. That's more than twenty five miles from here."

"Then what are we going to do?"

"You'll see soon enough."

Butler continued rowing, his arms mildly sore now. His face was damp from the thick fog and his legs felt like two pillars of ice. But the mission was almost accomplished. When he figured he was out far enough he took the EDF and pressed a button. A tiny light-emitting diode began to flash.

"What's that?" Natalia asked.

"I'm signalling our position to the submarine."

"Oh, a submarine is going to pick us up?"

"I told you that I wasn't rowing all the way to Finland."

He shipped oars and leaned back, looking at the black waves. Somewhere down there Captain Sinclair and his submarine had been waiting for his signal and now were homing toward it.

"I am a little afraid," Natalia said. "I wonder what will become of me."

"You'll go to America and we'll find you a good job. You'll have a car and a color television set like all other

Americans. You'll be very happy."

"But I miss Russia already," she said sadly.

"Life is hard and we must learn to adjust to new circumstances. You'll probably marry an American millionaire and live happily ever after."

"I'll never be happy, because I'm worried about my father."

"Your worrying can't help him. I told you that. He knew what the odds were when he decided to work with us. He was ready for this contingency, I'm sure. And he might even get out of it."

She shook her head. "I don't know."

There was a *swoosh* sound to starboard and they looked to see the nose of the submarine break through the waves a hundred yards away. Butler grabbed the oars again and rowed toward it. The submarine surfaced completely and lay on the water like a big black cigar. Its hatches opened and figures could be seen coming onto the deck.

"My goodness!" said Natalia.

Butler rowed toward the submarine, an old World War Two American model, upgraded and modernized by scientists from the Institute. As the rubber boat drew closer, a sailor threw out a line. Butler caught it and tied it to a cleat on the rubber boat's gunwale. A group of sailors pulled the rubber boat against the hull of the submarine. They threw down another line, and Butler handed it to Natalia.

"Hang on to it," he said. "They'll pull you up."

She gripped the rope tightly and the sailors pulled her to the deck of the submarine. Then they threw the rope to Butler and pulled him aboard. Lastly they pulled the rubber boat aboard.

Captain Sinclair was among the sailors on deck. "Glad you made it back, Butler."

"Thanks. This is Natalia Kahlovka."

"How do you do," said Captain Sinclair with a gracious bow.

"Hello."

"We'd better get below."

14

The sailors already were scrambling to the hatches, and Butler and Natalia followed Captain Sinclair into the conning tower and down the ladderwell. They descended into the submarine next to the periscope which was in its down position. They were surrounded by navigation officers and sailors sitting at electronic consoles with flashing, colored lights.

"Batten down the hatches," ordered Captain Sinclair, who had a white beard.

"Batten down the hatches," repeated Lieutenant Jordan, the executive officer of the submarine.

The sound of metal clanging could be heard throughout the submarine.

"Take her down to two hundred feet," Captain Sinclair said.

"Take her down to two hundred feet," Lieutenant Jordan repeated.

At the consoles, sailors pulled levers and threw switches. Butler hung onto a railing as the submarine angled downward. His body brushed against Natalia, still in her kerchief. She wore black wool slacks and a dark brown overcoat. The submarine leveled off.

"Bring her right forty-five degrees," Captain Sinclair said.

"Bring her right forty-five degrees."

"Steady as she goes."

"Steady as she goes."

Captain Sinclair turned to Butler and Natalia. "I imagine both of you will want to freshen up a bit. Lieutenant Jordan will show you to your cabins."

2

Butler stood before the mirror in his cabin and pulled off his stockingcap, revealing his black hair parted to the side. He took off his turtleneck sweater and the rest of his clothes, then stepped into the small shower stall to wash away the black camouflage on his face and hands. He had to scrub hard with soap and washcloth, because the stuff was designed to stay. But finally it came off and you could see his bushy eyebrows, square jaw, and roguish lips. People occasionally remarked that he looked like the young Clark Gable, and that always amused him. He didn't think he looked like Clark Gable at all. He thought he looked only like himself.

He came out of the shower, dried himself off, and brushed his hair. He thought it odd that he was getting dressed beneath the waters of the Baltic Sea. Science never ceased to amaze him. It could do anything. He put on a pair of dark-brown worsted slacks, a tan shirt, and a rust-colored sport jacket. Into his belt holster he stuck his Colt .45. He never went anywhere without it.

He left the room, walked down the narrow corridor, and knocked on the steel door of Natalia's cabin. He stood there, listening to the whirring sounds of the submarine.

The door opened a crack. Natalia stood there, wrapped in a robe, with damp blonde hair and freshly scrubbed face. "Hello," she said.

16

"Remember me?" he asked.

Her eyes searched his features. "So this is what Butler really looks like."

He smiled. "Uh-huh."

"Very nice," she said.

"Are you hungry?"

"As a matter of fact, I am."

"What would you like?"

"Anything."

"I'm glad you said that, because there probably isn't much of a selection aboard this submarine. I'll see what I can rustle up."

Butler continued down the corridor to the navigation room, where Lieutenant Jordan sat at a console, watching flashing lights. Lieutenant Jordan looked up as Butler approached. "Hello, Butler, how are you feeling?"

"I'm hungry, and so is Ms. Kahlovka. Can we get anything?"

"There's a cook on duty in the galley. Ask him to put something together for you."

Butler walked forward to the galley, feeling out of place among the uniformed sailors that he passed along the way. They all had been recruited into the Institute just as he had been. They were opposed to the military-industrial-CIA complex that dominated the so-called free world, and were equally opposed to the totalitarian dictatorships of Communist countries. The Institute was the only force in the world that tried to moderate between both extremes as it worked toward a better world of freedom and justice for everybody.

The cook sat in a corner of the galley reading a copy of *Popular Photography*. The galley was a small area with a grill, oven, workbench, and stainless steel refrigerators.

"What can I have to eat?" Butler asked.

The cook got up, took off his white hat, and scratched his head. "What do you want?"

"Something fast."

"Hamburgers all right?"

17

"Yes, and a salad. Enough for two. Some coffee and a glass of milk."

"Gotcha."

The cook took the food out of the refrigerator and proceeded to prepare it. Butler leaned against the bulkhead and wondered if Natalia really was who she said she was, and why her father had got nailed by the KGB. Although Butler knew from his own experience in such countries as Chile and Nicaragua that the CIA was a corrupt organization, he thought the KGB was even worse. But of course that was because the military-industrial-CIA complex was firmly in control in America, whereas evidently the commissars felt a little uneasy in the Soviet Union and therefore had to crack down harder.

In the jargon of the Institute, the military-industrial-CIA complex was known as Hydra, the seven-headed dragon of Greek mythology. It had corrupted and subverted governments throughout the free world in its never-ending quest for wealth and power, while in Communist countries the commissars had done basically the same thing. Hydra did it in the name of free enterprise, and the commissars did it for Marx, but it all was the same: in each region of the world a small ruling class was subjugating and brainwashing vast populations. And each ruling class was anxious to go to war against the other ruling class, using other people as cannon fodder of course.

The cook placed the food on a tray and Butler carried it back to Natalia's room, knocking on the door. She opened up, wearing a blue robe too big for her.

"Come in," she said.

He entered her tiny room and placed the tray on her bed. "I guess we'll have to eat here," he said, sitting on the bed.

"Yes, there's not much room," she replied, sitting on the other side of the tray.

He watched her move to the bed, and noticed that she was long-legged and svelte underneath the robe. Nice breasts too.

"What is this?" she asked, picking the top off a hamburger.

18

"Ground meat. A hamburger."

"Oh." She lifted it to her mouth and took a bite, chewed, looked at the ceiling, and swallowed. "Very good."

"I'll tell the chef."

He picked up his hamburger and bit off a chunk of it. They dined in silence, the submarine's engines providing background music.

"Where are we going?" she asked during her second hamburger.

"Sweden."

"What's there?"

"The Institute maintains its Scandinavian office near Stockholm. You'll be debriefed there, then I imagine they'll fly you to America and get you a good job. You'll have that color television set before you know it."

"I'd rather have my father back," she said ruefully.

"That could happen. You never know."

She shook her head. "No, they'll never let him go."

"Times change. Things happen. You can't be sure of anything these days."

"I hope you're right."

"The important thing is to keep hoping."

"I'll try," she said.

"By the way, I'll take those papers your father gave you. Where are they?"

"On the dresser."

Butler rose, went to the dresser, and picked up the papers. There were mathematical formulae written all over them, plus chemistry symbols. He folded the papers into his jacket pocket and returned to the bed, where he ate the final pieces of his salad and drank his milk. He always drank milk in preference to coffee because he was concerned about his protein intake. An active person like himself needed all the protein he can get.

"Mind if I smoke?" he asked, reaching for his pack of Luckies.

"May I have one?"

"Sure."

19

He held the pack out to her and she took one, which he lit. Then he took one for himself as she moved the empty tray onto the floor. Side by side, they leaned against the bulkhead, smoking their cigarettes.

"My head is spinning," she said. "Everything is happening too fast."

"You'd better get used to this sort of thing, because your next few days will be hectic. I don't suppose you've ever been out of the Soviet Union before."

"No. They don't let you leave unless you're a very high official, and maybe not even then."

"Your father left a few times though, didn't he?"

"Yes, to attend various international scientific conferences. At one of them he became part of the Bancroft Research Institute."

"He told you all this?"

"Yes. Two weeks ago. He thought the KGB was following him, and suspected the worst."

"Until two weeks ago you didn't know about his connection to the Institute?"

"That's correct. I'd never heard of the Institute, in fact."

Butler puffed his cigarette. "That's interesting."

"Why?"

"It just is."

"You think I'm some sort of KBG agent myself, don't you?"

"You could be."

"Those papers will prove my story."

"I hope so."

"Why do you hope so?"

"Because I'd hate to shoot you."

"Shoot me!"

"If you were a spy, that would be one way to handle you, don't you think?"

She shrugged unhappily. "I suppose so."

"But if you're what you say you are, I'm sure you don't have anything to worry about." He stood up. "Well, I imagine you're tired. We should be docking sometime in the late afternoon, so you'll be able to sleep late. Good night, and pleasant dreams."

"Good night, Mr. Butler."

"If you need anything, just knock on the wall. I'm in the next cabin. And there's one more thing. I'm afraid I'm going to have to search your clothing and then lock you in your room for the night. Until I know definitely who you are, I have to take normal precautions. I'm sure you understand."

"I suppose so," she said wearily. "My clothes are in the dresser over there."

Butler pulled out a dresser drawer and found the clothes. He searched through them, found the knife, and put it in his back pocket. In her shoulder bag there were only her cosmetics and a few identity cards. He tapped her shoes, but could detect no hollow spots.

"This is very embarrassing," she said, standing next to the bed, her arms crossed. "I've never had my personal clothing searched by a man before."

"It's going to get worse," he replied, turning around, "because now I'm afraid I'll have to conduct a quick search of your person."

"My person!"

"Yep. If there was a lady aboard I'd ask her to do it, but there isn't I'm afraid. Hold out your arms, please."

"What are you going to do?" she asked, her brow wrinkled.

"I'm going to search your person, I told you."

"How?"

"I shall feel with my hands for hidden weapons, radios, or what have you."

She sighed. "Perhaps it will be easier on both of us if I just remove my robe, so that you can look instead of touch."

"If you prefer."

"I suppose I must learn to be strong."

"That's true."

"This is as good a time as any to begin," she said, untying the belt that held her robe together. The robe fell open; he could see the valley between her breasts, her flat white

21

stomach, and the honey-colored hair at the junction of her legs.

"This is very embarrassing," she said.

"For me too."

"I think you're enjoying it."

"In a way I am, and in another way I feel like a lecher."

"You look like one. Well, here goes." She removed her arms from the sleeves of the robe. Peeling it off, she tossed it onto the bed and stood blushing before him, her hands behind her back.

He looked at her firm young breasts, their rosebud tips, her narrow waist and long delicious legs. He wanted to take her in his arms, throw her onto the bed, and ravish her with wild abandon, but he was a professional and he tried to be businesslike.

"Turn around," he said coldly.

She turned around, and he saw the mouth-watering curvature of her buttocks, her graceful back, and those long legs again.

"Turn around again."

She spun and faced him, her eyes downcast. "May I put on my robe now?"

"Yes. Sorry about all this. See you tomorrow." He headed for the door.

"Wait a moment," she said.

He looked at her again, and felt weak in his knees. She was shivering, but made no effort to put her robe on.

"What's your hurry?" she asked.

"Hadn't you better put your robe on? I think you're cold."

"I'm not cold."

"Then why are you shivering?"

"Because I feel strange. To be standing here naked with you looking at me is ... well ... exciting."

"It certainly is."

"Do you feel excited too?"

"I certainly do."

"How?"

He smiled, and now he was the nervous one. "I thought it was very erotic."

"So did I."

"Did you like it?"

"I think I did." She blushed redder, and now the color extended to her strawberry nipples. "You don't see me putting my robe on, do you?"

He moved toward her, put his hands on her shoulders, and pulled her closer. Their lips touched and their tongues found each other. She entwined her fingers in his hair and he ran his hands over her shoulders to her slim waist and curvaceous buttocks. She rubbed her little garden against his stiffening phallus.

"I think I'm going to take my clothes off so that you can search me," he said.

"Since you searched me, it's only fair that I should be able to search you."

He took off his jacket, shirt, and slacks. He kicked off his shoes and socks and pulled down his shorts.

She looked him up and down. "Turn around."

He turned and stood, wondering what a woman would look at.

"Face me."

He turned again and moved toward her. She looked confused, not knowing what would happen next, and he picked her up in his strong arms, carried her a few steps to the bed, and placed her on top of it. Then he lowered himself on top of her, searched for her lips, and felt her writhing underneath him. She mumbled a few words in Russian, then fastened her lips to his and raised her pelvis. He reached down to her soft wetness and ran his fingers through her hidden treasure. She clasped his phallus with her long elegant fingers and squeezed it hard, stroking back and forth. Then she aimed it at her target and pulled him in slowly. The sensation made his toes curl.

"Do you still think I'm a spy?" she murmured into his ear.

"Lady, at this point I don't give a damn who you are," he

replied as he took her buttocks in his hands and commenced pumping.

She wrapped her legs around his waist and met him stroke for stroke, as the submarine plowed its way through the Baltic Sea.

3

The next afternoon, the submerged submarine entered a fiord about fifty miles south of Stockholm. In the navigation room, sailors sat at their consoles making certain the vessel would not collide with the underwater rocky cliffs. Captain Sinclair stood with his arms wrapped around the pods of the periscope, looking at the white stone building that was the Scandinavian headquarters of the Bancroft Research Institute.

"Down periscope," he said, stepping back.

"Down periscope," repeated Lieutenant Jordan.

"Take her down to fifty feet."

"Take her down to fifty feet."

"Steady as she goes."

"Steady as she goes."

Captain Sinclair and Lieutenant Jordan walked to the sonar console, where a cathode screen showed an electronic picture of the underwater cliffs around them. Between the cliffs was a luminous outline of the submarine.

"Bring her right ten degrees," said Sinclair.

"Right ten degrees."

The submarine headed straight for the cliff on which the Institute building sat. If you were observing the submarine from an airplane, it would appear that the submarine would crash into the cliff, but instead it entered a wide tunnel cut into the cliff.

"Reduce speed to one knot," said Sinclair.

"Reduce speed to one knot."

Captain Sinclair studied the cathode screen. It showed the tunnel widening into a large docking area.

"Take her up," said Captain Sinclair.

"Take her up."

The bow of the submarine angled upwards, and Butler held the railing for support. He wore his trenchcoat over his slacks and sportcoat, and beside him Natalia stood in the slacks and coat she'd worn yesterday when he'd picked her up on the Russian coastline.

"This is home," Butler whispered in her ear.

"I'm afraid," she replied with a shudder.

"If you're who you say you are, you have nothing to worry about."

"But they say many an innocent person has gone to the gallows."

"We have very sophisticated electronic devices, dear. They'll know whether you're lying or not."

She looked at him in consternation. "But sometimes even lie detectors make mistakes."

"Not ours, dearie. Compared to ours, ordinary lie detectors are like axes from the Stone Age."

The submarine leveled off. Sailors scrambled up the ladderwells and opened the hatches.

Captain Sinclair held his hand out to the ladderwell. "After you," he said to Butler and Natalia.

Natalia climbed the ladderwell, and Butler followed her up with Captain Sinclair behind him. They rose into a huge cave lit with rows of flourescent lights along the walls. Sailors tied the submarine to cleats and shackled a gangplank from the walkway along the stone wall to the submarine. When the gangplank was secure, Sven Lundborg of the Institute boarded the submarine. He was slim, 28 years old, and wore a snug double-breasted blue suit. Butler, Natalia, and Captain Sinclair were climbing down from the conning tower, and Lundborg looked quizzically at Natalia.

"Welcome back, Captain," Lundborg said to Captain Sinclair, shaking his hand. "How'd it go?"

"No problems on my end."

"Welcome back, Butler."

"Hello, Sven. This is Natalia Kahlovka. Her father was picked up by the KGB yesterday, but she got out."

"How do you do, Ms. Kahlovka."

"Hello."

Sven put his arms around both their shoulders. "Why don't we all go upstairs and get debriefed."

They proceeded down the walkway to a corridor at the end of which was an elevator. Getting on, Sven pressed the top button and they rode up to the eighth floor of the building. They got off the elevator and walked down a sparkling white corridor. Through windows they could see the sun shining on the fiord below.

"You'll be speaking with Mr. Bjork," Sven said to Natalia. "His office is right here."

Sven opened a door and they entered a small office with a secretary typing behind a desk.

"You wait here, Butler," Sven said.

"Right." Butler looked at Natalia. "Good luck, kid."

"Will I see you again?"

He smiled. "I hope so, but one never knows."

Sven opened another door and led Natalia into Bjork's office. Butler stood beside the secretary's desk and lit a Lucky.

The secretary, the archetypal Swedish beauty with blonde hair and blue eyes, looked up at him. "Mr. Butler, you know you shouldn't smoke. You know it's bad for you."

"Everybody's got to have a vice, and this one is mine, dearie."

She looked at him incredulously. "I'm sure you have other vices, Mr. Butler."

"Like what?"

"I'd rather not say."

"Oh, go ahead and say."

"No."

She turned back to her typewriter. Sven returned from Bjork's office. "Come with me down the hall, would you, Butler?"

"Why, sure."

Butler followed Sven down the corridor to an office similar to the one they just were in, where a blonde secretary sat at a desk. Sven opened the next door and led Butler into his office, a spartan room twenty feet square with huge picture windows overlooking the fiord.

"Have a seat, Butler."

Butler sat on one of the leather chairs in front of the sleek wooden desk. Sven dropped into a chair behind the desk. The sunlight gleamed on his thinning golden hair and sharply chiseled features.

"You don't mind if I tape this, do you, Butler."

"Of course not."

Sven pressed a button on his desk. "Go ahead. Take it from the time you left the submarine."

"I left the submarine around one o'clock in the morning and rowed to shore. There was a thick fog, just as we'd anticipated. I encountered one Soviet patrol boat on the way in, but it didn't see me. When I was close to shore I signalled with my EDF and received an answer. I rowed to shore and signalled again. The young woman who's with Mr. Bjork came running to me. She said she was Natalia Kahlovka, and that her father had been picked up earlier in the day. We got in the boat and rowed back to the submarine. Another patrol boat, or maybe it was the same one, came close, but didn't see us. Finally I signalled to the submarine and it surfaced nearby, taking us aboard. Later, Ms. Kahlovka expressed concern on numerous occasions that I didn't believe she really was Dr. Kahlovka's daughter. I searched her for weapons, hidden radios, and the like, but found nothing. She appears rather distraught, which is understandable regardless of who she really is. I guess that's all."

"Think for a few moments. Something else might occur to you."

Butler sat and looked at the rocky crags through the window behind Sven. "I can't think of anything that might be of official interest."

"How about something that might be of unofficial interest?"

"Well, we had sexual relations and spent the night together."

Sven sighed. "Do you have to turn all your operations into orgies, Butler?"

"It wasn't an orgy—there only were the two of us. As I said, she was extremely distraught and it seemed like the appropriate thing to do under the circumstances."

"Why is it that on so many of your operations the appropriate thing to do is for you to have sexual relations with the nearest young woman?"

Butler threw up his hands. "C'mon, Sven. Life is much different in the field than it is here in the tranquillity of your office. We operational agents often find ourselves in strange situations where we must make difficult on-the-spot decisions. Sometimes we get into strange states of mind where improbable things suddenly happen. Ms. Kahlovka and I were a bit frazzled by our experience. Somehow we fell into bed together. I hope you won't think badly of her because of it."

"I don't think badly about her, but I can't help wondering about you. I'm concerned that your lack of constraint in sexual matters might get you into trouble some day."

"We were on the submarine, Sven. There was no danger."

"I think you ought to get married, Butler."

"I have been married. It didn't change anything. That's why she divorced me."

Sven sighed. "Can you think of anything else that you might want to tell me?"

"No."

"If you do, let me know."

"Of course."

"Well, I suppose you'll require a few days to unwind. The weekend's coming up, so why don't you report to my office on monday at nine. The girl should be debriefed by then, and we'll know which way we're headed."

"Good."

"Have a good time, Butler."

"You too, Sven. My regards to your wife and kiddies."

Butler got up and walked out of Sven's office. He made his way down the corridor to the elevator, took it to the main floor, left the building, and crossed the gravelled parking lot toward another office building that also was a dormitory for Institute people who were in transit or on temporary duty, like Butler.

The building was rectangular and white. Butler went inside, took the elevator to the fourth floor, and walked down the corridor to his room. Unlocking the door, he entered and took off his trenchcoat, hanging it in the closet.

He walked to the window and looked down at the fiord. Gulls swooped and shrieked and the sun glittered on the waves. He took out a Lucky and lit it up, inhaling out the side of his mouth. The operation was finished and he was debriefed. Now he could relax at last. He sat on a chair that had wooden arms and a fabric covered seat and back, puffing the cigarette.

He'd been in Sweden only a month, and it still was a strange place for him. Most of his CIA duty had been in the hot-blooded countries of South America, and Scandinavia was a striking contrast to that. Here the people were calm, rational, and sensible. They were extremely polite, and you didn't see children starving in the streets. The people enjoyed a high standard of living, higher in some respects than in the U.S.

He'd been sent here because his last operation had been in South America, and the Institute thought he'd better get out of that hemisphere for awhile. He'd been seen by certain members of Hydra, and it was thought that would impair his effectiveness. What was the opposite of Latin America? Scandinavia. And here he was. He'd hoped for Hong Kong or Tokyo, but he liked Scandinavia so far. The seafood was marvelous, the cities were clean, and the women were out of this world.

He decided to drive to Stockholm and maybe find an American movie to see. Getting his trenchcoat out of the closet, and putting a wide-brimmed brown fedora on his head, he left his room and went down to his car, an old Saab Sonnet, painted red with a white stripe down the side. It was a two-seated roadster and the top came down, which Butler loved. He folded the top into the trunk, got in the cockpit, and started it up. He drove down the road, showed his I.D. to the guard at the gate, and soon found himself on the highway to Stockholm, buzzing along at 60 kilometers an hour.

As he passed forests turning bronze and gold, he remembered Sweden's foremost tourist attraction which he hadn't seen yet. It was the Wasa, a preserved 17th century man-of-war that sank on her maiden voyage in 1628, only a few hundred yards from the spot where she'd been launched. It lay in mud for over three hundred years and then in 1961 was raised with pontoons, restored, and housed in its own museum. Should be an interesting thing to see, he thought, something to write home about if he had anybody at home to write to.

Museums were a good place to pick up pretty girls. Maybe he'd find one today, he thought, motoring over the winding road.

4

It was Monday morning at eight-thirty. Butler drove his Saab into the parking lot of the Institute complex and stopped in his slot. He got out, pulled up the top, and closed the doors. A cigarette dangling out the corner of his mouth, he made his way to his room, took off his shirt, and shaved quickly.

All had not gone according to plan. There had been no pretty blondes in the Wasa Museum, but that had been all right with him, because the ship was spectacular and it was enjoyable looking at it without somebody to distract him. Afterwards he went to Gamla Stan, the old section of Stockholm, and stopped in a little restaurant for herring sandwiches and beer. Two crazy young French tourist girls happened to be sitting at the next table, and one thing led to another. He spent part of the weekend in their hotel room with them, and the other part seeing the sights of Stockholm with one of them on each of his arms. It had been most enjoyable, but now he was tired and spaced out. Somehow he had to pull his brain together for the nine o'clock meeting with Sven Lundborg. He looked at his eyes in the mirror. The whites were covered with red worms. He grimaced, went to a dresser drawer, and took out a pair of sunglasses.

He crossed the parking lot, and gulls swooped through the air above his head. The sun was low on the horizon, casting a weird golden glow over everything. Entering the main building, he took the elevator up to Sven's office.

The secretary looked up as Butler entered. "He's expecting you. Go right in."

Butler opened the door to Sven's office. Sven sat behind his desk, looking over some papers. He didn't appear to have gotten much sleep either. He glanced at his watch.

"Right on time, I see," he said.

"On time, every time," Butler replied with a smile, collapsing into a chair.

"We've been looking for you all weekend. Where the hell were you?"

"In Stockholm. Didn't you say I could take the weekend off?"

"Yes, but the shit has hit the fan, as you Americans say. Mr. Sheffield has flown in all the way from California to take control of the situation. He wants to see you right away. He's in Mr. Bjork's office."

Butler walked down the corridor to Bjork's office. He was in a mild state of shock from knowing that Sheffield was there. Sheffield was executive director of the Bancroft Research institute, Numero Uno himself. Something very big must be going on if he was here taking command personally.

He opened the door to Bjork's office and saw Ms. Allen, one of Sheffield's secretaries from the Institute headquarters in Big Sur.

"Hi, Ms. Allen. I understand the chief is waiting to see me."

"Let me check." She picked up the phone on her desk, pressed a button, and mumbled into it. "Go right in," she told Butler, hanging up the phone.

Butler opened the door to the inner office and stepped inside. All the windows had been covered and it was pitch black except for the area where the desk was. A lamp on the desk sent a beam down to some papers being fondled by two hands, and behind the hands was the shadowy figure of

Sheffield. Butler had never seen him, and as far as he knew no one else had either.

"Hello Butler," said Sheffield in a voice that established his age somewhere in the fifties or sixties. "Have a seat."

Butler sat in the darkness and crossed his legs. A lamp on the ceiling bathed him in golden light.

"A very serious situation has developed, Butler," Sheffield said. "Very, very serious."

"That's what Mr. Lundborg told me. Can you tell me what it is?"

"Of course I can, and I shall. Because we want to put you to work on it right away. We want to drop you inside the Soviet Union before the week is out, and sooner if possible."

Butler stiffened in his chair. "Drop me in the Soviet Union? That'll be very risky. Soviet security is tighter than a drum. Even the CIA can't operate in the Soviet Union. Whenever they'd tried to run an agent in the Soviet Union, the agent always got caught."

"Well," said Sheffield softly, "we're not the CIA, are we? We know things that they don't know. We have a plan to eliminate a lot of the risk for you. But first let me give you some background. As you know, the Institute is trying to prevent various maniacs in the huge power blocs from destroying the world, and the best way to do this is to insure that the major blocs have a general parity in weapons and technology. As long as one side can expect a devastating retaliation if it starts a war, it will hesitate to do so. This has been the status of the so-called Cold War until now. But now something has happened to change the balance of power drastically. The girl, Natalia Kahlovka, has brought us some truly unsettling information. Do you know what smart weapons are?"

"They're missiles guided to their targets by laser beams," Butler answered. "They can be surface-to-surface missiles, air-to-surface, surface-to-air, or air-to-air. If the gunner can hold the target in his sights, the missile will hit its target."

"Correct," said Sheffield. "And as you know, these smart weapons have changed the face of modern warfare. In the

34

1973 Middle East War, more tanks were thrown into battle than any other engagement in history except for one near Kursk on the Russian front during the Second World War. Due to the use by both sides of smart weapons, more than three thousand tanks were destroyed and more than 600 aircraft were downed. No longer can hordes of tanks attack an enemy with impunity. The new generation of smart weapons make that impossible. In fact, thanks to smart weapons, both the United States and the USSR can cut their arms budgets drastically. Smart weapons used for defense have made most offensive weapons obsolete. Tanks, aircraft, and battleships have become absurd. But of course, everybody continues to build them in preparation for another World War Two, or whatever. We've learned long ago that military intelligence is to intelligence as military music is to music."

"Until Friday," Sheffield continued, "we believed that both sides of the cold war had an arsenal of smart weapons that would discourage attacks from each other. But young Ms. Kahlovka has brought us terrifying news. The Russians have devised, or are in the process of devising, an instrument that confuses laser beams. It sets up an electronic microwave field that causes laser beams to bounce back in the direction from where they were aimed. That means the missiles aimed by the laser beams will come back to friendly lines and explode, and an attacking army can advance without serious opposition. As you can readily perceive, this is a most dangerous situation because it might encourage the Russians to stage a pre-emptive strike against Western Europe or the United States before these latter countries can develop a counter-measure to the new weapon, which we have code-named the 'Doom Machine.'"

"Therefore," Sheffield went on, "we must stop the Doom Machine. There are two possible ways to go about it. The first is to sabotage the plant—wherever it is—that is manufacturing the Doom Machine. The second is to obtain the specifications for the Doom Machine and make it available to all the countries of the world that don't have it.

That ought to even everything up again and bring us back to square one."

Butler leaned forward in his chair. "I thought the girl brought the plans out with her."

Sheffield chuckled. "If only she had. Unfortunately she only brought out the most general information, but that's better than nothing. At least, now we know that the Doom Machine exists, and can do something about it. As I said earlier, we are sending you into the Soviet Union toward the end of this week, if you agree to go, of course."

"But I don't speak Russian. I'll be a sitting duck. They'll pick me up in two minutes."

"Cover is everything, Butler. With the right cover you could go into the jaws of hell and come out clean. This is what your cover will be: you will be a deaf-mute, a poor pathetic creature who's cared for by your sister, who will speak for you, take care of you, and will be your constant companion. No doubt you're wondering at this point who this sister will be. Well, it will be none other than Natalia Kahlovka, the girl you brought out of the Soviet Union."

"You trust her?" Butler asked.

"Yes. Don't you? She passed all our tests."

"I don't know. I suppose she's all right if she passed all the electronic tests. You can't fool the machines, can you?"

"We don't think so."

"Then I'll start trusting her."

"Good. We'd like you to begin your preparations immediately. Although you will be a mentally retarded deaf-mute, we would like you to learn to read Russian and understand it. You can't pick up very much in three days, but you'll get the rudiments. We also want you to learn sign language, and you'll be indoctrinated in Russian life and be taught from maps and photographs about what to expect in the city of Moscow, which is where you're going, by the way. The Doom Machine is being developed in the Vasilkov Munitions Plant there. We have a mole in Moscow, a person we've never used. Her name is Sonia Barsovina, and she is a doctor. We recruited her five years ago at a medical conference in London. She's been sitting on ice, just waiting to go operational. And she speaks English. As far as we know, she lives alone. She is a lesbian, we believe."

"Good grief," Butler said.

"You don't like lesbians?"

"They usually don't like me."

"I suspect that's because you make advances toward them. If you don't make advances to Sonia I'm sure you'll be all right. We're not sending you into the Soviet Union to get laid, if you'll pardon the expression."

"It's pardoned."

"Good. Any questions so far?"

Butler scratched his head. He didn't like the idea of going into the Soviet Union, because it seemed extremely risky. If he could point that out, maybe he wouldn't have to go.

"I don't have a specific question at this point, but just a matter that we ought to consider. We must assume that the KGB is searching for Natalia right now. They're liable to pick her up as soon as she sets foot in the Soviet Union."

"We've thought of that. Natalia's blonde hair will be dyed black, and she won't be going to Leningrad, where presumably they're looking for her. She has never been to Moscow, and on top of that you won't be going to Moscow south from Leningrad, but north from Volgograd, formerly Stalingrad. They won't be expecting her to come from that direction, and once you're in Moscow, of course, you will merely melt into the population."

"What about identification papers?"

"You'll have the best that master forgers can produce. You will be Boris Noginsk, and Natalia will be your sister. You both are orphans. She has just graduated from secondary school, and has taken you, her poor sick brother, out of the lunatic asylum in Volgograd to go to Moscow to visit your dear cousin, Sonia Barsovina. When you arrive in Moscow you will telephone her and say, or I should say that Natalia will say, 'Do you remember your cousins from Stavropol?' That is the code sentence that Sonia has been waiting to hear for five years. She will reply, 'I don't remember any cousins from Stavropol, but I believe I do have some in Grozny.' Then you can talk more or less freely and make arrangements to meet. Any other questions?"

Butler shook his head. "This is going to be a very dangerous operation, Mr. Sheffield."

"You don't have to go if you don't want to. I'm sure we can get somebody else."

"Perhaps it would be better if you sent somebody who could speak Russian."

"We have people who speak Russian, but none of them are as skilled as you are in covert operations. You happen to be just about the best person we have on that score, Butler. But I'm sure we could find somebody else."

Butler waved his hand. "I'll go."

"I'd appreciate it. It's a very important operation."

"I can see that."

"The fate of the world might possibly hang in the balance here."

"That's usually the case, isn't it?"

"I'm afraid it is." Sheffield paused for a few moments. "Do you think you'll be able to get along all right with Natalia?"

"I don't see any reason why not."

Sheffield coughed. "I understand you've had sexual relations with the girl, is that so?"

"Yes."

"She's very young, you know."

"She's not that young."

"Perhaps she's not young in relation to the women you normally associate with, but nineteen isn't very old."

"She's only nineteen?" Butler asked, surprised.

"Yes, and they can be very romantic and emotional at that age."

"Some are very cold and brutal at that age," Butler pointed out.

"But this one isn't American. She's Russian. Their society isn't as loose as ours."

"I think I can handle her."

"Try to bear in mind that you're on an operation of great importance, and not a little sexual lark, all right? I know she's pretty and all that, but keep the mission uppermost in your mind. Do you think you can?"

"Of course I can."

"Good. That will be all, Butler. Report to Mr. Ishevsk on the second floor. He'll be your Russian teacher, and Mr. Donaldson, formerly of the Old Vic company in London, will give you a little class in makeup and disguise, just so you can brush up on those things. Professor Henry will teach you sign language. Any questions?"

"Not that I can think of offhand."

"Good luck, Butler."

"Thank you, sir."

"And I'd like to express my gratitude to you for agreeing to undertake this most important and dangerous mission."

"That's okay, sir. Anytime." With a wink, Butler rose and walked out of the office.

"Butler?" asked Sheffield.

Butler stopped and turned around. "Yes?"

"Um, we haven't told the girl much about us, for security reasons. Don't tell her anything she doesn't have to know, all right?"

"I thought you trusted her. You said she passed the electronic tests."

"It's always good to be cautious. We don't want her to know anything she doesn't have to know. Compartmentalization. You understand."

"Does she know who we are?"

"Only in the most superficial way."

"Then let me ask you something: how do you know that the papers she delivered were written by Doctor Kahlovka?"

"We know they were in his handwriting, but of course they could have been written under coercion."

Butler nodded. "So in other words, she might not be what she appears to be."

"The same might be said of any of us. But we can't let that stop us from taking appropriate action."

"Are you going to tell the Americans about the Doom Machine?"

"No, because it might panic them into starting an immediate war in the hope that the Soviets don't have the Doom Machine completely finished and operational yet. We'd better not notify them until we can give them the plans on a silver platter."

"Tricky situation, isn't it."

"The trickiest. Any more questions?"

"Not at the moment."

"If any crop up, come see me. Until then, you'd better get moving to Mr. Ishevk's Russian class. We don't have much time, you know."

"I know," Butler replied, heading toward the door once more.

5

Butler studied the Russian language with Ishevsk and brushed up on makeup and costume with Donaldson. Professor Henry taught him sign language, and in the evening he and Natalia attended a briefing by a Mr. Slobodskoy, a defector from the Soviet Union, who told them about life in the Soviet Union—what to expect, how to proceed, and so forth.

It was ten o'clock at night when the briefing was over, and Butler walked with Natalia back to the dormitory compound where they both were staying. He'd noticed that she'd been casting certain glances at him during the briefing, and he thought he knew what the glances meant, particularly when she put her arm around his waist in the parking lot.

"I am so happy to see you again," she said, smiling at him.

He looked into her innocent, nineteen-year-old face and it beamed with love or lust, or both, for him. "I'm happy to see you too, dear."

"I was afraid that you had gone away someplace. I am in love with you, you know."

He looked at her as they neared the building. "I didn't know."

"No?"

"No."

"After all that happened between us, you didn't know?"

"No."

"You think I am that way with every man I meet?"

"How should I know?"

She removed her arm from his waist. "You have just insulted me," she said sadly, and began to sulk.

"Sorry."

He opened the door to the dormitory and once again cursed himself for screwing around on the job. He was going into the Soviet Union with her on a mission of great importance, and already they were having emotional problems. They walked down the corridor to the elevator and he pressed the button. She looked at him sadly out the corners of her sloe eyes.

"I don't mean anything to you at all," she said tragically.

"I can see that."

"You do. Of course you do."

"I am just helping you with your spy business, and you have used my body once. That's all."

The elevator came and they stepped inside. Two scientists in white coats already were aboard, riding up from the basement laboratory evidently. Butler didn't want to continue the conversation in front of them, so he got off with her at her floor.

"I think we'd better have a talk," he said.

"Good."

They walked down the corridor to her room, and a young woman and man in jeans passed by. Natalia opened the door and Butler followed her into her room, which basically was like his room, resembling a modern, moderately priced hotel room. She turned on a lamp and took off her coat; he handed his trenchcoat to her and sat on a chair near the window. Hanging the coats in the closet, she returned and sat on the bed.

"Now listen," he said, "we're going out on a very dangerous operation together and we'd better have an understanding right now so that we don't have any trouble later. In my line of work, I've seen many people die, and I've

42

come close to getting knocked off myself on numerous occasions. In order to survive emotionally, we can't let ourselves get too attached to people, and that's why I appear uninvolved to you. Please don't take it personally. You're a very nice person. Okay?"

"But I am in love with you," she said.

"That's nonsense."

"Perhaps to you, but not to me."

"Love is a fantasy. You're having a fantasy about me. It's not real."

"Not real?"

"No."

"You're sure of that?"

"Quite sure."

"Oh."

She arose from the bed, a half-smile playing on her lips. Kicking off her shoes, she unbuttoned her blouse and slowly, tantalizingly, peeled it off. Her firm young breasts flopped into view, and he stared at her pointed brown nipples and his mouth began to water. She unzipped her skirt and pushed it down. Now she stood before him, clad only in plain white cotton bikini underpants. But on her they looked like the most expensive and exotic garment ever made. She pushed them down too and walked toward him, kneeling between his legs, reaching for his swelling erection.

"Is this real?" she asked playfully.

"That is very real."

"It's not a fantasy?"

"Not at all."

"But I thought you said everything between us is a fantasy."

"There is a difference between love and lust," he said.

"Love is a fantasy, but lust is real?"

"Very real."

"Oh, I see."

She unzipped his fly and took out his big pink rod.

"And what is this?" she asked, wagging it in the air.

43

"If you don't know by now, I could never explain it."

"Sometimes it's difficult to know the difference between love and lust," she said.

"That's true."

She squeezed it. "Maybe love and lust are both the same thing?"

"I doubt it."

"Why?"

"Because love is more intellectual than lust."

"All I know is that I'm mad about you."

She lowered her head and brought his penis into her mouth. He felt chills run up and down his spine. Through slitted eyes he saw her head moving rhythmically up and down. Her tongue flicked at him, and with her free hand she moved her hair out of the way.

I'm going to pay for this someday, he thought, resting his hand on her bobbing head.

6

On Friday, Butler and Natalia were flown in an Institute jet plane from Stockholm to Istanbul. They were driven from the airport to the docks of the city, passing slums, beggars, and business men in fez hats. The downtown area was an odd mixture of old Byzantine structures and modern buildings. Some of the women wore western dress, but most wore long, black, native dresses.

The docks were like the docks of any major city—piled high with cargo against a background of tethered ships. There was a bazaar where merchants sold copper utensils and fresh vegetables. At the end of the docks was a small marina area where the yachts of the wealthy were tied up and being worked on by swarms of servants.

The limousine stopped in front of this marina area. Butler and Natalia got out, followed by Abdul Kefir, the associate director of the Institute's office in Istanbul. Abdul wore a double-breasted suit and a maroon fez, and had a big handlebar mustache. He was a chemical engineer and an expert in desalination technology.

Carrying a suitcase, Kefir led them down the pier to a white yacht used by the Institute of oceanographic research. They boarded the boat and were greeted by Captain Josh Wilkerson, thin as a rail and very tanned. Pleasantries were exchanged and Kefir wished Butler and Natalia good luck, then left the boat.

Captain Wilkerson introduced Butler and Natalia to the members of the boat's crew, then lines were cast off and the boat sailed through the Bosporus into the Black Sea. It was a bright sunny day and the air was heavy with oil and salt. The boat, named the *Windsong*, was sixty feet long and loaded with electronic gear for oceanographic work and the monitoring of the Soviet fleet in the Black Sea area.

Butler and Natalia stood on deck, the wind ruffling their hair. They watched Istanbul recede into the distance, then turned toward the Soviet Union, which they couldn't see yet.

She looked at him and smiled. "You look so handsome there, with the sun on your face and the wind in your hair. No wonder I'm in love with you."

"Young girls fall in love so easily," Butler replied with a chuckle.

"You always make fun of me."

"I cannot take young girls seriously, I'm afraid. They're too romantic and sentimental. That makes them silly."

"You think I'm silly?"

"In a way."

"I'm not that much younger than you."

"You're only nineteen. That's very young. But you're very charming and nice. I do love you, in my own special way."

She raised her eyebrows. "What way is that?"

"I can't explain."

"Why can't you explain?"

"Because words are too crude to describe the subtlety of my feeling."

She harumphed. "It's so subtle that it's probably nonexistent."

"Oh, come on. We have more important things to talk about."

"To me there is nothing more important than love."

"That's because you're a silly young girl. I think you should start getting used to thinking of me as your deaf-mute retarded brother."

"The retarded part will be easy," she said with a smile.

7

It was midnight in the middle of the Black Sea. Butler was in his cabin, standing before the mirror. He wore baggy black pants, a worn black-and-white-checkered overcoat, and a gray wool cap with a visor. He hadn't shaved for three days, and a stubble covered his features. Russian identification papers were in the pocket of his shirt, along with an old fountain pen that concealed a tiny laser gun. If you pressed the clip it would emit a beam that could melt metal or burn a hole through a human body in seconds. It was the only weapon he carried. Some rubles were in his pocket, and taped to his thigh was a set of picks that he could use to open most ordinary locks.

There was a knock on his door.

"Yes?" said Butler.

"Time to come up on deck," said the voice on the other side of the door.

"I'll be right up."

There was a valise on the cot, and Butler picked it up. He opened the door and stepped into the corridor, seeing Natalia leave her cabin. She was wearing the same outift she'd had on when he'd picked her up near Tallinn a week ago.

"Ready to go?" he asked.

"Uh-huh."

"Scared?"

"Not very."

They climbed the ladderwell and went up on deck. It was a clear night and a half-moon floated in the sky, shining on the smooth waters of the Black Sea. Captain Wilkerson and one of his officers were on the starboard side of the deck, looking into the distance with binoculars. He glanced at Natalia and Butler as they approached.

"Hello folks," he said, returning his gaze to the sea. "The sub should be along any moment now."

Butler put his arm around Natalia's shoulders and looked out at the sparkling water. It was peaceful and lyrical. When this operation was over, Butler thought he'd like to take a nice long vacation in this exotic part of the world. Maybe rent a villa on the north coast of Turkey. Go to little cafes and watch the belly dancers. He felt Natalia tremble.

"You okay?" he asked.

"I think so."

"If you're having doubts, this is the time to get them off your chest."

"I have no doubts."

There was a sudden swooshing sound as the black submarine broke through the surface of the water fifty yards away. Captain Wilkerson turned to his bridge and pointed toward the submarine. The *Windsong* veered toward starboard as hatches were opened on the deck of the submarine and sailors spilled onto the deck.

The submarine and research ship converged toward each other. When they were close, lines were thrown from one to the other and bumpers were thrown over the side. A catwalk was fastened between them and Butler stood beside it with Natalia at his side.

"Good luck," Captain Wilkerson said, shaking Butler's hand.

"Thanks."

Captain Wilkerson kissed Natalia on the cheek, then Butler and Natalia climbed onto the catwalk and made their way to the deck of the submarine, where Captain Sinclair was waiting alongside Lieutenant Jordan.

"Welcome aboard," Captain Sinclair said, shaking their hands quickly. "We'd better get below immediately. The Russians patrol these waters, you know."

Butler and Natalia climbed up the conning tower and then descended the ladderwell into the control room of the submarine. The sailors sat at their consoles, watching the blinking lights. You could hear other sailors descending ladderwells and running along the inside of the submarine.

Captain Sinclair stood beside the downed periscope, and Lieutenant Jordan was at the main control console.

"All the hatches are secure, sir," Lieutenant Jordan said.

"Take her down."

Lieutenant Jordan repeated the order, then pressed buttons and flicked switches on his console. The front of the submarine tilted downward and Butler knew they were submerging quickly. Captain Sinclair gave the order to level off, and Lieutenant Jordan passed it along. Finally the submarine was moving slowly and silently beneath the Black Sea.

"Well, here we are again," Captain Sinclair said to Butler. "You really get around."

"Yes, we're dropping people off and picking them up all the time. Let me take you to your cabins."

Captain Sinclair led Butler and Natalia to the front of the submarine where the torpedo tubes had been during the Second World War, but whose space had been converted into cabins. Butler went inside his cabin, put the valise on the bed, and sat down. For the rest of the night and most of tomorrow, the submarine would travel across the Black Sea, into the Sea of Azov, and up the Don River to Volgograd. In about twenty-four hours Butler and Natalia would get into a rubber raft and row toward shore. They'd land in the Soviet Union and danger would be their constant companion.

Butler took out a cigarette and lit it up. Puffing, he considered that he'd been on many dangerous operations

49

during the course of his career as a spy, and before that he'd been a Green Beret in Vietnam. He'd looked Death in the face many times and still was alive to tell about it, but he always figured that some day in some strange land the bullet was going to come with his name on it, and it would be the end of the line for him. At the beginning of every operation he wondered if this would be the one, though he was still alive. Yet who knew what hand Fate would deal tomorrow in the Soviet Union?

Butler blew smoke into the air. This kind of thinking couldn't bring you anywhere except down. He wondered what Natalia was doing. It probably wasn't a good idea to leave her alone too much. Her fears might run away with her. She was an emotional girl. And besides, if he was going to die tomorrow, it might be a good idea to get laid one last time tonight.

He rose and took off his hat and coat. Then he left his room and walked down the corridor to Natalia's room and knocked on the door.

"Who is it?" she asked.

"Me."

She opened the door, and was in a serious mood. "What do you want?"

"How are you feeling?"

"All right, I suppose."

"Worried?"

"A little."

"Can I come in?"

"If you want to."

She held open the door and he walked into her tiny room. The covers on her cot were turned down; evidently she'd been getting ready for bed.

"Want a cigarette?" he asked, holding out his pack.

"Thank you." She took one.

He lit it with his Zippo, and reminded himself to leave the Zippo and the Luckies behind when he left tomorrow.

"Would you like to talk?" he asked.

"About what?"

"About anything you like. Your hopes, fears, dreams, predictions about the future, evaluations of the past, and so forth."

"Are you horny?"

"What makes you say that?"

"Why else would you be here? You really don't care about me."

"Of course I care about you."

"You think I'm a child."

"That's true, but I care about you anyway."

"All you want me for is my young body."

He moved closer to her. "What's the matter with that?"

"I am more than just a body," she said reproachfully.

"Of course you are. You have a brilliant mind and you have beautiful thoughts."

She laughed ruefully. "You must really be horny."

"Just a little."

"Yesterday you told me I shouldn't love you so much."

"That's true—you shouldn't."

"And yet today you come lusting after my body."

"There you go again—getting lust and love mixed up. Listen, I'm getting tired of this runaround. I think I'll go back to my cabin and get some sleep."

"No, no," she said quickly, darting between him and the door. "You don't have to leave."

"I don't."

"No."

"I thought you were mad at me."

"I am, but not that mad."

"I can't figure you out."

"Don't try. It's too much for your puny little mind." She looked at the bed. "There's not very much room."

"We won't need very much," he said, unbuttoning his shirt.

She came to him and put her arms around his waist. "You know, when we get into the Soviet Union we won't be able to do this anymore."

"I'm sure we'll find a way."

"Don't be so sure."

"Then this might be our last one for awhile, huh?"

"Yes."

"Then we'd better make it good."

She rested her cheek against his chest. "With you, it's always good."

"What a sweet thing to say. What a nice girl you are."

"Not that nice," she said, reaching between his legs.

He hugged her and kissed her lips, tasting the sweet nectar, and he knew she really was a nice girl no matter what she did or said.

Or so he hoped.

8

Late the next day the submarine passed Taganrog and entered the Don River. It moved slowly in the middle of the channel close to the bottom as huge tankers and cargo ships rumbled past overhead. Captain Sinclair and Lieutenant Jordan were in the control room throughout the night, monitoring their progress on the electronics systems.

At two o'clock in the morning they entered the Tsimlyansk Reservoir, on which the city of Volgograd was constructed. Then they angled toward shore. The drop-off point would be a stretch of barren coastline ten miles from Volgograd near a huge lumber factory.

At three-ten the submarine surfaced 400 yards offshore, and the rubber boat was put over the side. Butler went into it first, then he helped Natalia down. Their faces were blackened and they wore black camouflage outfits over their clothes. They carried no radio and no weapon except Butler's laser pen, which Natalia didn't know about. His set of picks was taped to his thigh. In the boat were two oars and a shovel. Butler sat at the oars and Natalia sat in front. It was a cool autumn night and her teeth chattered. She hugged herself as Butler began to row toward shore. The sea gurgled as the submarine sank below the surface, and Butler was alone with Natalia near Volgograd.

She turned around and looked toward shore. "It is so good to be home," she said.

"Oh come on," Butler said, pushing the oars.

She turned around and faced him. "You don't believe me?"

"Yes, I believe you. You're sentimental enough to miss this giant slave camp."

"You are talking about the government, and I'm talking about the land and its people. This is my Mother Russia. It is a great country. You will see."

"Yeah."

Butler pushed toward shore. To his right he saw piles of lumber sitting in the moonlight, and to his left was a scrubby little forest. He steered toward the forest, and it was easy going because the surface of the reservoir was still. Silently the rubber boat glided toward shore and struck sand. Butler jumped out and pulled the boat onto the beach, then Natalia got onto the dry sand.

They knelt beside the boat and waited for a few seconds, listening for movement or signs that they'd been detected. Then they dragged the raft up the beach past the high water mark to a spot near the edge of the woods. Butler took the shovel and began digging a hole while Natalia went back and smeared their tracks with her hands.

Butler perspired heavily as he dug the hole, but he knew this was a crucial part of the operation. Many spies had been caught in the past because their boats were found, thus prompting a search. They'd been in too much of a hurry to dig a deep hole, but Butler wasn't in that much of a hurry. His shovel bit into the soft sand and slowly scooped it away as Natalia deflated the boat.

Finally he had a hole that was as deep as his chest. He threw in the deflated boat, stomped on it, then threw in the oars and the shovel. Next he and Natalia took off their black camouflage suits and threw them in the hole. Finally Butler took damp washcloths out of plastic packages and wiped the black paint off his and Natalia's face and hands. He threw the washcloths into the hole, then he and Natalia got down

54

on their hands and knees and pushed the sand into the hole. When it was filled they smoothed the sand around. By morning the beach would look like it was before they got there, and the rubber boat would never be found.

So far so good. They crossed the scrubby forest and came to a two-lane highway. Turning right, they walked on the shoulder to Volgograd, passing stacks of lumber and then the lumber mill working at night, steam and smoke shooting from its chimney and lights glittering within its windows. Occasionally a big truck thundered by, but no one took any special notice of them. They appeared to be two typical Russian peasants on their way someplace.

By dawn they reached the outskirts of Volgograd, a huge city with a population of nearly a million, originally built in 1589 at the juncture of the Don and Volga Rivers. It had nearly been destroyed in 1942, but now was an important center for oil refining, lumbering, and the manufacture of heavy machinery. They walked past factories and housing projects for workers, and slowly reached the downtown area, where Communist art and slogans were on billboards and walls instead of the advertisements for products one saw in the so-called free world.

The citizens of Volgograd were on their way to work, and Butler thought they looked pretty much like Americans, except that their clothes weren't fashionable. The women didn't wear much makeup and Butler thought some of them were quite pretty, but he behaved himself and fumbled along beside Natalia, letting her hold his arm while he rolled his eyes and pretended to be a slackjawed idiot.

Finally they reached the railroad station, a big boxy concrete building. They went inside and made their way through the crowds to the ticket counter, where Natalia bought two tickets to Moscow. Communist art and slogans were everywhere, like regular advertisements in an American railroad station, and Butler had to admit that the Communist stuff didn't look any worse, and perhaps in the long run was better because it didn't coax you to buy things that you didn't need. Butler tried to keep an open mind about such things. He knew that closed minds produce opinions that are biased and therefore worthless.

Natalia led him down to their gate and he saw people looking at them, probably sympathizing with the pretty girl who was taking care of the bumbling idiot. He was tempted to laugh, but permitted himself only an idiotic giggle. Finally they reached the gate, and Natalia explained to him in sign language that they had to wait 90 minutes. So they sat in a waiting room area and an old lady beside Natalia started talking to her while Butler looked at the crowds swarming through the railroad station.

The old lady went away, and Natalia told Butler in sign language to stay put. She went to the newstand in the middle of the floor and bought two magazines giving him one to look at. Butler thumbed through the magazine, looking at pictures of Soviet actresses, cosmonauts, politicians, and ballet dancers. There also were farming scenes, factories, and one photo of Russian soldiers marching in a big public square. That reminded Butler of the Doom Machine and the mission he was on. If the military maniacs had their way, there wouldn't be anything left of the world.

Something prompted Butler to look up. He saw two policemen walking through the train station, looking at people. A sensation of paranoia fell over him as he wondered if maybe through some weird event the rubber boat had been found and now the authorities were searching for Natalia and him. But the police walked right by and he relaxed; they probably were looking for a petty thief or somebody who murdered his mother-in-law, not Butler the master spy.

At the appropriate time, Natalia motioned for him to get up and, taking his arm, led him through the passageway and down the stairs to the train, a sleek chromium express. They boarded the train and sat on two seats with Butler close to the window. A young Army officer sat across the aisle from Natalia and struck up a conversation with her. Butler felt jealous and realized the girl meant more to him than he'd thought. Was he falling in love with her? he asked himself. Could be.

The train filled with people, leaving few empty seats. Finally it rumbled out of the station. It travelled underground for a long way, and then suddenly came up into the sunlight amid an area of housing projects. A few old men and women walked about. Butler figured most people must be at work or school.

The train sped into the countryside, passing fields that seemed to go on forever. It reminded Butler of the wheat country in Montana and the Dakotas, except that this land was flat. The train buzzed through the farmland, and Butler began to think that the land was endless, and that he was trapped inside a symphony of scenery that would go on forever.

Next the train came to a region of forests and rivers, and again Butler thought it would never end. Late in the afternoon a man came through the car selling sandwiches, and the Army officer who'd been talking to Natalia offered to buy some for her and her crazy brother, but she insisted on paying for them herself.

Butler watched a landscape of trees pass his window as he munched on a sausage sandwich and drank, of all things, a bottle of Pepsi-Cola. After his meal, Butler looked out the window at more fields.

The train came to the city of Voronezh and stopped for a half hour. Butler and Natalia went out on the platform to stretch, and the Army officer followed them, talking to Natalia, probably asking for a date. Butler wanted to punch his lights out, but that would never do.

They returned to the train and soon were heading north again. Dusk was falling and soon it was completely dark. Butler asked in sign language where the toilet was and Natalia told him. He slid past her and walked down the aisle, doing his idiot act. He had to wait outside the toilet for a drunk to come out, then went in and took a leak. Coming out, he returned to his seat and asked Natalia if he could have a cigarette. She asked the Army officer who gladly handed her the whole pack, but she just took two, and the Army officer passed her his book of matches.

Butler liked the cigarette. It reminded him a little of the ones French peasants smoked: strong and tasty. Natalia resumed her conversation with the Army officer as the car became dark. Some people put lights on above their heads so they could read, but Butler decided to get some rest. After finishing his cigarette he closed his eyes and tried to doze off, but wasn't very successful. He'd never had much success trying to sleep sitting up. Natalia stopped talking to the officer and cuddled against Butler a little. He was tempted to nuzzle in her breasts, but that wouldn't do either.

Bells clanged throughout the night, and lights flashed by the window. Occasionally Butler would open his eyes to see little towns in the middle of nowhere, with no one on the streets and only a few lamps burning. And then it was back into the country again, the fields and forests, the tractless space that was Russia.

9

The train pulled into Moscow Station at five o'clock in the morning. The passengers sleepily disembarked and the officer gave Natalia his phone number while Butler looked at the tracks and wondered if that was the exact spot where Anna Karenina jumped to her death. He also wondered what Tolstoy would think if he saw Russia today. It'd probably blow his mind.

Natalia said goodbye to the officer and then took Butler's arm and walked him to some telephone booths. *I'm going to call Sonia now*, she told him in sign language.

He nodded approval.

She went into a phone booth and dropped in a coin. Then she dialed the number. It rang and rang on the other end. Finally somebody picked it up.

"Hello?" said a sleepy female voice in Russian.

"Sonia?" asked Natalia.

"Yes," Sonia said cautiously.

"Do you remember your cousins from Stavropol?"

There was silence on the other end for a few seconds, then, "I don't remember any cousins from Stravopol, but I believe I do have some in Grozny."

"There are two of us," Natalia said with urgency. "Can we come over now?"

"Um, I have a friend with me, but that's all right. It isn't every day that my cousins from Stravopol come here."

"We are using the names Boris and Katerina Noginsk."

"Ah, yes, my father's sister's children," Sonia said to fool whoever was with her. "How nice to hear from you. Do you know how to get here?"

"We have subway directions."

"Good. I'll make some coffee. See you soon."

Natalia hung up the phone and looked at Butler. In sign language she said, *We're going over there now, but she has someone with her.*

Who?

I don't know. Maybe a lover.

They took an escalator down into the subway station which Butler considered palatial compared with the ones in New York. Passing a mirror, he looked at himself and saw a grungy fellow in a crooked cap who need a shave. They boarded a subway train and rode for awhile, then got off, boarded another, and rode that one for awhile. Then they left the train and climbed stairs into the fabled city of Moscow.

They found themselves in a neighborhood of tall apartment buildings made of concrete, all identical. The architect must have drawn them in his sleep. Street lamps still were on and the sun rose in the east. Natalia led him to a building and they went inside to the elevator, pressing the button. When it came it disgorged seven sullen men and three sullen women. Then Butler and Natalia got on, riding to the seventh floor. They walked down the corridor and knocked on a door.

There were footsteps on the other side and Butler wondered if something had gone wrong. A KGB agent was waiting with his gun out, but the door was opened by a beautiful young woman with platinum blonde hair worn short. Her skin was pale as snow.

"Sonia?" asked Natalia in Russian.

Sonia nodded and smiled. "Yes, dear."

They hugged and kissed with great feeling, considering that they'd never seen each other before in their lives. Natalia introduced Butler and dumbly he smiled. Sonia looked at him curiously, then said loudly in Russian, "How wonderful it is to see my dear cousins from Stravopol again." Then she invited them inside and closed the door.

"Are we alone?" Natalia asked, looking around the small room. There was a bed, easy chair, and desk with another chair in front of it.

"Yes," said Sonia, wearing a diaphanous blue gown.

"I thought you had someone here with you."

"I told her my cousins from Stravopol were on the way over, so she left."

Natalia looked at Butler. "He is an American and does not speak our language. We should speak English from now on, but very softly, because he is supposed to be a deaf-mute."

"I see," said Sonia in accented Russian. She looked at Butler and whispered, "Your costume is very good."

"So is yours."

She blushed. "This is a very small apartment. The only place I can offer you to sit is the bed." She indicated it with her delicate hand, and Butler wondered what she'd been doing on it all night with her girl friend.

The bed, big enough for two to sleep comfortably, was against the wall, and they all sat on it, leaning their backs against the wall. Butler was in the middle, with the women on either side of him.

"What is it you want me to do?" Sonia asked.

Butler answered her. "We want you to put us up for awhile, while I try to get some information on a new weapon being developed at the Vasilkov Munitions Plant."

"Ah, I have a friend there!" Sonia exclaimed.

"You do?"

"Yes. Grushenka Kutozov. She is a doctor at the Vasilkov Munitions Plant. We both are members of the Moscow Doctors' Union."

"Will she cooperate with us?"

"Not with you, but with me. We are...very good friends."

From the hesitation in her voice, Butler realized that Sonia and Grushenka had made it together.

"Was she the friend of yours who was here last night?"

"No, that was another friend of mine," Sonia replied, embarrassed.

"How soon can you talk to her?"

"Tonight, if I can reach her during the day today. What do you want me to find out?"

"There is a research project being supervised by a Professor Lebaykin. It has to do with a new microwave weapon that can change the power balance in the world and thereby bring about a situation where the Soviet Union might feel emboldened to launch World War Three. We must get copies of the plans so that we can distribute them throughout the world and thus restore the balance of power."

"I'll ask her about it tonight."

"Can you trust her?"

"Yes, we're very close," Sonia said. She looked at her watch. "I had better get ready for work. It wouldn't be good for me to be late. Especially now that you're here."

"Go ahead," Butler said.

Sonia got off the bed, took some clothes out of the closet, and carried them to the bathroom.

There was a knock at the door.

Sonia stopped on her way to the bathroom and looked curiously at Butler and Natalia.

Butler pointed to the door and whispered. "You'd better answer it."

Sonia draped her clothes over a chair, went to the door, and opened it up. Two men in overcoats and slouch hats were there, and the one in front held out a badge of some sort. Sonia's face drained of what little color it had. Butler's heart shuddered as he looked at Natalia, who was smiling.

The two men strolled into the little room. "Is there someone here named Natalia Kahlovka?" one of them asked in Russian.

"That is I, Comrade," Natalia replied, getting off the bed

and walking toward them. "Place these two spies under arrest."

Butler didn't understand Russian but he knew something awful was going down. The two men took out guns and pointed them at Butler and Sonia.

"You're under arrest!" one of the men said in Russian.

Sonia nearly fainted. Natalia looked at Butler and smiled triumphantly. "Let me translate for you, fool," she said. "You are now a prisoner of the Soviet Union. These two men are KGB agents, and so am I. Hereafter you will refer to me as Captain Novoshakhtinsk."

"I don't think I can pronounce that."

"You'll learn soon enough, capitalist pig." She turned to Sonia. "Put your clothes on, sex degenerate. You're going to jail." Then she looked at Butler again. "Perhaps you're wondering how I notified the KGB?"

"I imagine you told that Army officer."

"Correct. I had you so blinded with lust that you didn't even suspect me."

"That's not true exactly, dear. We always suspected you, but we had to play along with you. The fate of the world hung in the balance. And by the way, you give great blow jobs."

Sparks flew out of her eyes. She stormed toward him and punched him in the mouth, but he was a big fellow and didn't flinch. "Pig!" she screamed.

"Whore."

She punched him again, and this time a small trickle of blood appeared at the corner of his mouth. Butler decided it was time to stop taunting her. Sonia, meanwhile, was putting on a dress and coat over her nightgown. Her hands were trembling and Butler felt sorry for her. She'd been a mole for five years, and now on her first assignment got nailed before she even left her apartment. They'd send her to a labor camp in Siberia and that would be the end of her, because she was a frail, delicate thing, so pale and ethereal.

"Why don't you let her go?" Butler asked Natalia. "She hasn't done anything."

Natalia held her finger in the air. "But she was going to do something if she had the chance. She was going to strike a blow against the worker's state which educated her and made her a doctor."

"Give her a break, Natalia."

"I'll give her a break. I'll break her dirty revisionist neck!" She looked at the two men with guns. "Take them away," she ordered.

10

A black paddy wagon was waiting out front, with a Zim automobile behind it. Butler and Sonia were herded into the back of the paddy wagon, and Natalia got into the car with the two KGB agents. The paddy wagon drove away, with the car close behind it.

Butler and Sonia sat facing each other on the benches in back of the paddy wagon as it rattled over the streets of Moscow. There was a tiny window in back.

"I'm awfully sorry about this," Butler said.

"It's not your fault," she replied in a voice barely above a whisper. "This is a dangerous world that we live in, and we have to expect this sort of thing if we take a stand against the cruelty and madness. It is better to die a wolf than a lamb."

"Hold on—nobody said anything about dying. We might get out of this yet."

She shook her head. "Once people disappear into the Gulag system, they're never seen again."

"There's always a chance," he protested.

She shook her head sadly. "I'm afraid not," she shuddered as a sob passed through her body.

Butler moved to her side of the bench and put his arm around her shoulder. "Don't give up hope, whatever you do. I'm considered a very smart fellow. I'm sure I can get us out of this somehow. I can't believe that a man like me will have to spend the rest of his life in the Gulag Archipelago." He hugged her closer to him.

She dropped her cheek on his shoulder. "Ah, it's so sad to be so young and to be put in prison."

"Be strong, Sonia. I'll think of something."

"You don't know how difficult the Russian prison system is. There's no way out unless you have influential friends, and we have no influential friends."

"Don't give up hope," he said. "I'm telling you that I'll think of something."

She laughed ruefully. "You're just saying that to cheer me up, but don't worry about me, I can take the truth."

"I'm not saying it just to cheer you up."

"Then you're saying it just to cheer yourself up?"

"I'm saying it because I'm a very capable person. I've broken out of jails before."

"But never in Russia."

"A jail is a jail."

"Well, good luck," she said, skepticism still in her voice.

"I'll tell you what—let's bet on it. I'll bet you a hundred rubles that I get us both out."

She shrugged. "All right—one hundred rubles. Why not? If everyone else is mad, we might as well be mad too."

He took her slender hand in his and shook it. "It's a deal," he said.

They sat jouncing around on the bench, his arm around her shoulders and her hand in his. Their bodies rubbed against each other, and Butler began to get turned on. He was on his way to prison with a lesbian, and in the forefront of his mind was a desire to have sexual relations with her. He laughed at his foolishness and lust.

"What is funny?" she asked, turning her pale, beautiful face toward him.

"You wouldn't believe it," he replied.

"I'd believe anything at this point. Why are you laughing."

"Well, here we are on the way to prison, and all I can think about is that I'd like to make love to you right now."

"What!"

66

"I told you that you wouldn't believe it."

She took his arm off her shoulders and moved away from him, looking at him with fear and suspicion. "How can you think of something like that at a time like this?"

"You're very lovely."

She sighed. "You Americans are crazy. I've always heard it, but now I know it's true."

"I'm not crazy at all. The problem is that you don't realize how attractive you are to men. You've been sleeping with women too long."

"Now that's enough!"

He pointed his finger at her. "I'm going to get your goodies someday. You just mark my words."

She squealed and moved farther away from him. "Don't touch me."

"I'm not going to touch you now, but someday I'm going to get you."

"Never."

"Never say never."

She shook her head and raised her chin in the air. "Never!"

"I'll bet you another hundred rubles."

"Where are you going to get all those rubles? You're going to jail, you idiot!"

"We're getting out before long. You'll see. Come on, let's shake on it." He held out his hand.

She looked at it. "You're crazy."

"Come on—a hundred rubles."

Pinching her lips together, she grasped his hand. "It's a bet," she said.

"A bet that you're going to lose."

She looked at the roof of the paddy wagon. "I must be even crazier than you."

"You are if you think you're going to win this bet."

The paddy wagon stopped suddenly, and they both fell to the side. The rear door clanged open and Natalia was standing there with the two KGB men and two uniformed guards.

"Okay—out you two!" Natalia snarled.

"Natalia, how you've changed," Butler said sadly.

"OUT!" she screamed.

"Why, you're becoming a hysterical woman." He looked at Sonia. "After you."

Sonia crouched toward the door and jumped off the paddy wagon, and Butler followed her. They were in front of a stone wall ten feet high, behind which were gray stone buildings.

Sonia raised the back of her hand to her forehead. "The Kaluga Prison," she said in dismay.

"What's the Kaluga prison?"

Natalia laughed sadistically. "What's the Kaluga Prison?" she asked. "It is the most notorious KGB prison in the Soviet Union. It's the place where we find out what we want to know." She looked at the guards. "Take them away."

The guards marched Butler and Sonia to a gate, showed identification, and were admitted to a cobblestoned prison yard. The morning sun gleamed on a vast number of concrete buildings with cupolas and spires on top. Butler thought it looked like photographs he'd seen that showed the inside of the Kremlin. Natalia and the two KGB men walked behind them, and Butler thought about what a weird, twisted little girl Natalia must be.

They entered the main reception office of the Kaluga Prison. There was a uniformed official behind a raised desk and several armed guards standing around. Natalia barked some orders in Russian, and the official began filling out papers. Natalia signed them, and then she ordered guards to take Butler and Sonia to their cells.

As Butler was being led out of the room, he turned to Natalia and said, "How could you do this to me, after all we've meant to each other?"

"We meant nothing to each other, you idiot," she replied, looking at him haughtily.

"How did you beat our lie detector machines?"

"That's none of your business, fool. Get moving!"

Butler waved to Sonia. "See you on the outside, kid."

Sonia frowned as she was led through another door. Two guards grabbed Butler by the arms and marched him out of the reception room into the dank, labyrinthine corridors of the notorious Kaluga Prison. From afar they heard men groaning, sobbing, and snoring. There was little light, and the air smelled of disinfectant.

They went down stairs, through passageways, and then up stairs. Butler became disoriented, not able to place where he was in the prison complex, which he realized was the general idea behind taking him on this circuitous route. Finally, in what appeared to be the very bowels of the prison, they entered a narrow corridor lined with cells. A guard opened one of the doors, and the other guard pushed Butler into a cell.

"Hey, take it easy there," Butler said, brushing himself off.

They mumbled to each other, locked the door, and walked away. Butler sniffed the air and scratched his head, looking around. Here I am in jail again, he thought. He'd been jailed numerous times throughout his career, and always had managed to get away. This jail should be no exception, right?

He sat on the cot attached to the wall and looked around. There was a commode in the corner and that was it. Your standard lousy prison cell—bars facing the corridor and stone walls all around, a cup of soup and a slice of bread every once in a while.

Previously he'd been imprisoned in South America, and the jails weren't so tough down there. But a Russian jail might very well be different, and in fact probably was. He'd been acting bluff and confident to cheer up Sonia, but actually he didn't feel that optimistic. Even if he got out of this cell, how could he get out of the prison, how could he get out of Russia?

There had to be a way. When they'd searched him superficially, they'd neglected to take his little laser pen. It was a harmless-looking little plastic thing and it had got him out of scrapes before. Presumably it would again. But he'd have to do it right, because he knew they wouldn't give him a second chance.

He hadn't slept much on the train the night before, so he

thought he might as well go to bed and try to repair his strength for the ordeal that lay ahead. He hoped Sonia was all right, as he lay down on the hard wooden cot. He didn't feel very lustful anymore. She must be in a state of shock, poor kid. Well, that's the way the cookie crumbles.

He closed his eyes and went slack on the cot. Things have to get better, he thought, because they sure as hell can't get much worse.

11

He was awakened by the sound of his cell door being opened. Two hulking guards entered his cell, and one of them grabbed him by the shoulder.

"Come with me," the guard said.

"Where to?"

"Do as you're told, and stop asking questions."

The guards marched him through a series of corridors and passageways that seemed to go deeper into the ground. Finally they reached a brightly lit corridor lined with steel doors. Somebody screamed horribly behind one of the doors, and Butler thought, Uh-oh, it's interrogation time.

The guards knocked on one of the doors and it was opened by Natalia dressed in a uniform consisting of a light brown skirt and dark brown jacket. Underneath the jacket she wore a white shirt with a black tie.

"Hi sweetheart," Butler said, still bluffing and still trying to get them off guard.

"Clown," she muttered.

She stepped out of the way and the guards pushed him into the room. There was a chair with shackles on it, a desk, and a few more chairs. Standing in the corner smoking a cigarette was a tall man with a shaved head, big ears, high cheekbones, and small chin. His eyes turned down at the corners, he wore a male version of Sonia's uniform, and he looked like the meanest, nastiest person Butler had ever seen in his life.

"Hi there?" Butler said cheerily. "Who might you be?"

The man looked at him through slitted eyes. "A more significant question might be, 'Who are you?'" He had a guttural Russian accent and his lips curled down in contempt as he spoke.

"Who me?" Butler asked. "I'm just an American tourist, and I can't help wondering what I'm doing here."

"You are a spy!" the man shouted.

"Who me?"

"Sit down!" He pointed to the chair with shackles.

Butler sat gingerly in the chair and looked with disapproval at the shackles. "Surely you're not going to put those things on me, are you?"

"Only if you make it necessary for us to do so."

"I wouldn't dream of that."

The man scratched his nose. "Permit me to introduce myself. I am Major Alexei Ospenko of the People's Secret Police, better known to you perhaps as the KGB. And this is Captain Natalia Novoshakhtinsk, whom you have already met."

"Howdy, folks." Butler looked at the guards standing by the door. "Who're they?"

Ospenko waved his hand in the air. "They do not matter. Are you comfortable?"

"No."

"That's too bad, because that's as comfortable as you're going to get." He took a package out of his jacket. "Cigarette?"

"If you please."

Butler took a cigarette, and Ospenko lit it with a match. Inhaling, Butler looked at Natalia. She had her hair done up in a bun behind her head, and it was back to its natural color of honey blonde.

Ospenko commenced pacing back and forth in front of Butler, holding his cigarette at chest level. "Perhaps we can begin by having you tell us who you are."

"My name's Butler, and I'd like to speak to someone at the United States Embassy, if you don't mind."

"We do mind. You will speak to us only. If you tell us what we want to know, then perhaps we will consider letting you go. What are you doing in the Soviet Union?"

"Sightseeing mostly. You know, Saint Basil's Cathedral, Lenin's Tomb, the Kremlin. All the hot spots."

Ospenko stopped pacing and shook his head. "Mr. Butler, if you keep playing around we'll chop off your fingers and feed them to the pigeons. Now, supposing you tell us what is this Institute that you work for?"

Butler smiled. "What Institute?"

Natalia cleared her throat. "That place where I was in Sweden."

"Oh, that place. By the way, Natalia dear, you really ought to leave your hair down. It's not becoming at all the way you have it now."

Ospenko turned suddenly and whacked Butler across the mouth. "Stop fooling around!"

"I'm not fooling around." Butler touched his mouth, and his fingers came back with blood on them. The game was getting rough.

"The question was," Ospensko said, "what is this Institute you work for?"

Butler realized he'd have to string them along a little; otherwise they'd beat him to death. "Well, it's a scientific organization," he admitted.

"What does it do?"

"Scientific work."

"Like spying on the Soviet Union!"

"Oh, no, the Institute wouldn't do anything like that."

Ospenko puffed his cigarette and looked Butler in the eye. "Is it not true that you are a CIA agent, and that you are just using this Institute for your cover?"

"Of course not. What a ridiculous suggestion."

"Ridiculous is it?" Ospenko stomped to the desk, opened the top drawer, and took out a folder. He carried the folder to Butler and took a picture out of it. "This is a photograph of you leaving the U.S. Embassy in Ecuador in the year 1971, when you were a case officer with the CIA. And here," he said, taking another photo out, "is a picture of you in downtown Caracas when you were the deputy chief of the CIA station there. And this one shows you in Chile, again as the deputy chief of station, in the days before the Allende regime was overthrown by fascist elements. How can you deny that you're a member of the CIA?"

Butler thought it over. He decided it would be better to admit being a CIA officer than surrender any information on the Institute. In point of fact, he had been a CIA man for many years and was an accomplice to many dirty deals such as the overthrow of Allende, but the CIA had fired him because he was opposed to so many of their dirty deals. That's when the Institute recruited him.

"Okay, I'm a member of the CIA," Butler said.

"Hah!" exclaimed Ospenko, looking at Natalia.

She smiled. "I knew it all along," she said with a wave of her hand. "They thought they were fooling me with all that talk about the Institute, but I knew they were CIA, the fools. They thought they were clever, but I was more clever than they." She walked toward Butler and kicked him in the shin, causing him to howl in pain. "Why, this idiot even thought I loved him! Can you imagine such a ridiculous thing?"

"Of course not," chuckled Ospenko.

Butler held his aching shin with both hands. "After all, how could *you* love anybody?"

"Exactly," Natalia said, strolling around proudly with her hands on her hips.

"But I made you come," Butler said.

She stopped and stared at him. "What was that?" she asked.

"You heard me. I made you have many orgasms."

Natalia looked at Ospenko. "Don't believe him," she said with desperation in her voice.

"What's this?" Ospenko said, raising his eyebrows.

"I made her come," Butler said.

Ospenko turned to Natalia. "He did?"

"Of course not!" she protested, waving her fists through the air. "I only was acting! How can you think that I'd enjoy something like that?"

"Pssst," Butler leaned over to Ospenko. "She enjoyed it."

"I did not!"

"Yes she did," Butler insisted. "You know how it is, Ospenko. A man of the world like yourself can always tell when a woman is faking it or not, right?"

"Right," agreed Ospenko.

"Well, she wasn't faking it."

"No?" asked Ospenko, looking at Natalia.

"Of course I was faking!" she insisted, her face becoming red. "What do you think I am. It was purely tactics and tradecraft. Why, I had the poor fool so much in love with me he didn't know what he was doing."

"I was never in love with you," Butler replied, not sure if he was lying or not.

"Perhaps I should have said that I had you crazy with lust."

"That's not true either."

"You told me during our last night on the submarine that you felt lust for me. Are you lying then, or are you lying now?"

"I felt lust for you at that moment, but I was by no means crazy."

"Hah!" she said, looking at Ospenko. "The truth comes out at last. He felt lust for me. I tricked him with my feminine wiles."

"And I made you come."

"You did not!"

Ospenko rubbed his forehead. "I'm getting tired of this foolishness," he said.

"I'm only trying to defend my professionalism," Natalia said, her nose in the air.

"Shut up."

"I made her come," Butler said again.

"You shut up too."

Butler looked at Natalia and stuck out his tongue. She

75

charged him and tried to whack him in the face again, but he was ready this time and caught her wrist in mid-air.

"That'll be enough of that," he said.

She turned purple and tried to hit him with her other hand, but he caught that one in mid-air too.

"Can't somebody calm this hysterical woman down?" Butler asked.

"Get away from him," Ospenko said.

Natalia stepped back. "I hate him," she said between her teeth.

Butler winked. "How can you say that to a man who made you come so many times?"

Natalia jumped at him again, but Ospenko caught her. "Stop behaving so foolishly!" he yelled.

Mollified, she cast her eyes down. Ospenko let her go, and she slunk into a corner.

"Now let's continue," Ospenko said, nodding his head from side to side. "We would like you, Mr. Butler, to sign a little confession for us. If you don't sign, we will kill you. If you do sign, we will let you go."

"Let me go where?"

"We will deliver you to the U. S. Embassy."

"No kidding?"

"I'm not kidding."

"Will you turn Sonia Barsovina loose?"

"Don't be ridiculous,"

"What's so ridiculous? I give you something, and you give me something. It's what's known as a square deal."

"You give us the confession, and we give you your life. That is the deal."

Butler scratched his head. "Let me think about this for a few minutes."

"Don't take too long. We haven't got all day."

Butler crossed his legs and leaned back in the chair. The moment of truth had arrived. If he didn't sign the confession they surely would kill him. If he did sign it they'd probably kill him anyway. He didn't have enough bargaining power to free Sonia or even insure his own freedom. Still, he thought he'd try. What the hell.

"Okay," he said, I'll do it if you turn Sonia Barsovina loose."

Ospenko shook his head. "I told you no on that already."

"Oh, come on. She doesn't know anything and she hasn't done anything."

"No."

"I won't sign the confession."

"We'll forge your name."

"Nobody will believe you."

"Some people will, because some people will believe anything."

"I'll make a speech for you. After I sign the confession I'll make a public speech and admit everything you want me to."

Ospenko pursed his lips. "You go on television?"

"Sure."

"Really?"

"Honor bright."

"You'll say anything?"

"Anything at all."

"Just for this girl?"

"Yes."

"Why?"

"I'm in love with her."

"In love with her? But she's a lesbian!"

"I'm crazy about lesbians. What can I tell you?"

"I don't know," Ospenko said, wrinkling his forehead.

Natalia stepped out of the corner. "She's only a mole. This was to be her first operation."

"But she should be punished!" Ospenko said, banging his fist into the palm of his hand.

Butler cleared his throat. "It's not good to be vindictive. And besides, look at it from the propaganda point of view. That will far outway one lesbian mole who never did anything."

"Let them go," Natalia said. "Who needs them?"

Ospenko ran his finger over his jaw. "Maybe you're right. Go fetch the girl, will you?"

"Yes sir."

Natalia marched out of the room, leaving Butler alone with Ospenko and the two guards. Ospenko paced back and forth like a caged lion in front of Butler, and the guards stood on either side of the door with their arms crossed.

"Tell me something," Butler said. "Do you really have microwave machines that can interfere with smart bombs, or was that just misinformation to confuse us?"

Ospenko chortled. "Do you really think I'd tell you that?"

"Oh, come on. It doesn't matter if you tell me."

Ospenko looked him in the eye. "It wouldn't matter if I was going to kill you, but since we're going to let you go, I'd rather that your country keeps guessing. There's nothing like terror to keep your enemies in line, wouldn't you say?"

"Ospenko, you're a dog."

"Watch you mouth, Yankee pig!"

"How about another cigarette, Ospenko old boy?"

Ospenko gave Butler another cigarette and light. Butler puffed it, trying to steel his nerves for the escape attempt which would commence shortly after Sonia was brought to the room. He hoped his laser pen was in good working condition, because if it wasn't, things were going to get very hairy in a little while.

Natalia returned to the room with Sonia, who looked more delicate and lovely than ever after her hours in prison. Her eyes glowed like hot coals and her skin was the color of cream. It looked as though it would break and spurt blood at the touch of a passionate man.

"Hi ya, Sonia," Butler said jovially. "How're they treating you?"

Sonia looked fearfully at Natalia and Ospenko. "All right."

"You and I are getting out of here just as soon as I sign a little confession."

"I do not believe they'll ever let us out of here."

"You're a pessimist. You must always look for the sunny side of life."

"There is no sun in the Kaluga Prison."

Ospenko cleared his throat harshly. "Enough of this chatter. Sit at the desk over here, Butler."

Butler got up and walked across the room to the desk, as all eyes followed him. He sat on the chair and looked at the confession. It was ten pages long, and as he glanced over it, it admitted to committing all sorts of heinous crimes against the Soviet state.

Butler chortled. "Gee, you didn't leave anything out, did you?"

"We in the KGB are most thorough." Ospenko reached to his shirt pocket and took out a pen. "You may use this."

"I have my own," Butler said with a smile, taking his laser pen out of his pocket.

"Let me see that!" Ospenko said, snatching the pen out of Butler's hand.

Butler's heart sank as Ospenko examined the pen. If Ospenko found out its terrible secret, Butler's brilliant career in espionage would come to a tragic conclusion.

Ospenko turned up his nose. "A cheap plastic pen for a cheap plastic man," he said contemptuously. He handed it back to Butler. "Here."

"Thanks very much," Butler replied, accepting it. It looked like his brilliant career in espionage wasn't coming to a tragic conclusion after all. "Would you mind if Ms. Barsovina stood beside me to sort of witness my signing."

Ospenko looked at the ceiling. "What a fool you are, Butler." He looked at Sonia. "Stand beside him, please."

Sonia, who was confused and jittery at this point, moved across the room and stood beside Butler, who was pleased to have her out of the way. Butler smiled at Ospenko and Sonia as he readied his pen, and they smiled back. The time had come for Butler to make his big move.

Still smiling, he pointed the head of the pen at Ospenko, and pressed the clip. A sliver of light shot out, striking

Ospenko in the chest. Before Ospenko could scream, he was dead. He slumped to the floor, but before he hit, Butler was aiming at Natalia and pressing the clip. Smoke poured out of her throat as she looked at him in disbelief, and before she fell he already was aiming at the guard at the left and burning a hole through his heart. The guard to the right tried to figure out what was happening all around him, but before he came up with the answer, Butler had put a hole in his head.

The four bodies crumpled to the floor. Sonia stared at them goggle-eyed. Her jaw dropped open and she raised her hand to her lips.

"It was nothing, really," Butler said modestly, putting his pen back in his shirt pocket.

He rose and walked to the body of Ospenko, who was lying on his back with eyes staring at the ceiling. Butler looked at the beauteous Natalia lying on her side, and was overcome by melancholy when he realized that they'd made love many times.

"How did you do it?" Sonia gasped.

Her question brought Butler back to his senses. "It was a little trick, a mere nothing," he said, looking at her. "Now we're going to try and break out of here. Put on her clothes, and I'll put on Ospenko's. We'll try to bluff our way through the gate."

She started to tremble. "I'm afraid," she whispered.

He walked toward her, grabbed her shoulders, and looked into her eyes. "Don't think—just do exactly as I say. It's your only chance. Now take off your clothes and put on Natalia's, understand?"

"I understand."

Butler let her go, returned to Ospenko, and started undressing him. Out the corner of his eye he watched Sonia undress. Even at this moment of extreme danger he could not prevent himself from being a voyeur. Her blouse came off and she wore a bra that held two healthy round breasts. Down came the skirt and he saw her long supple legs. She wore black underpants, the little rascal.

"What are you looking at!" she demanded.

"I was just making sure that you were doing what I said."

"I'm doing what you said. Stop looking at me."

Butler reluctantly removed his eyes from her and resumed removing Ospenko's clothes. Then he took off his own clothes and put on Ospenko's. The clothes were too tight for him and the red hole in the front of the shirt would pose a problem, but maybe he could cover it if he wore the necktie to the side. He strapped on Ospenko's belt, holster, and pistol. On a peg near the door was Ospenko's visored hat with red star in the center. Butler put it on and it fit just right. He turned to Sonia and asked, "How do I look?"

"You will strike fear into the hearts of any Russian," she replied, tucking in Natalia's blouse. "How about me?"

"The uniform's a little too big for you."

"You think anybody will notice?"

"Let's hope not. Put on your hat and let's get going."

"Going where?"

"Out of here."

She reached to the peg and put on Natalia's hat. Butler straightened it out for her and smoothed the front of her uniform.

"Okay," he said. "We're going to walk out of this room like two nasty, vicious KGB officers. If anybody says anything to you reply with the utmost contempt. Understand?"

"Oh, Lord."

"Let's go. Ready?"

"Uh-huh."

Butler opened the door and looked into the corridor. There was no one there. He motioned for Sonia to leave the room, then followed her out. They marched down the corridor in step and side by side. At the end was a door, which was locked. Butler pounded on it, a guard opened up and saluted, and Butler kept walking with Sonia at his side. There was a window in that corridor and Butler could see the prison yard. It was night. They came to a door leading to the yard, and a guard opened it up, saluting. They returned the salute and stepped into the yard.

"Do you know where we are?" she asked.

"Of course not."

They walked into the yard, and Butler looked around. He saw with dismay that the yard was surrounded by buildings. They were boxed in.

"Keep moving," he said. "We'll try that building over there."

They marched to the long gray stone building and opened the door. A guard standing just inside saluted. Down another corridor they marched, and through more doors. They came to the lobby of a building and Butler led Sonia out the front door, although he had no idea where that would lead.

They stepped into a yard covered with concrete, and straight ahead was the wall! A gate was about twenty yards away and they headed for it. A guard was standing on each side of the gate, and as Butler and Sonia approached, they saluted. Then they opened the gate.

Butler and Sonia stepped onto the sidewalk outside the Kaluga Prison. A car drove by on the street in front. The guards closed the gate behind them.

"Keep moving," Butler said. "Appear purposeful, like we know where we're going."

"Where are we going, by the way?"

"The American Embassy. Do you know where it is?"

"We're going in the wrong direction. It's the other way."

"Oh, shit, we can't turn around and go that way."

"Why not?"

"Because we won't look purposeful, and KGB agents are supposed to look purposeful. We'll have to go around the block."

A siren went off inside the Kaluga Prison. Butler and Sonia stopped and looked at each other.

"Uh-oh," Butler said.

Her face became streaked with fear. "What will we do!"

"Walk fast around the corner there."

Butler and Sonia quickened their pace as they headed for the corner. Four-story stone houses with peaked roofs were on the other side of the street, and in the distance against the night sky were the spires and domes of Moscow. As they approached the corner, two males in uniform turned and marched toward them.

Butler turned to Sonia. "Do we salute them, or do they salute us?"

"How should I know?"

"When in doubt, salute first. Let's do it."

"But I've never saluted before!"

"Just put your fingers against the brim of your hat and try to walk as if you've got a broomstick up your ass."

The two soldiers came closer, and Butler and Sonia saluted them. The soldiers saluted back and kept walking. More sirens were going off inside the prison walls. Butler and Sonia rounded the corner.

"Run!" he said.

They ran down the street, and came to an intersection. There was no traffic and no pedestrians. It must be very late at night, Butler thought. They took a left, and halfway down the block they saw a car parked at the curb.

"I think we're going to steal this car," Butler said, slowing down. "Do you know how to open the hood on one of these?"

"There's a latch near the steering wheel."

Butler tried the door, but it was locked of course. He unzipped his fly, reached inside to his thigh, and pulled off the tape with the picks. Selecting one, he picked the lock and opened the door. He found the latch near the steering wheel, pulled it, and the hood snapped open. He walked to the front of the car, lifted the hood, and looked at the wires. He found the ones leading to the ignition, pulled them from the firewall, and spliced them together.

"Get in the car," Butler said.

Sonia got behind the wheel and slid over to the passenger side. Butler slammed the hood shut and then got into the car, pulling the door closed. The sound of sirens grew louder, and Butler realized there were patrol vehicles outside the prison now.

"Uh-oh," he said.

"Start the car, you fool!" she hissed.

"Where's the starter button?"

"Over there. Don't you know how to drive a Zim?"

"Never drove one before."

"You'd better let me drive. Exchange places—fast!"

Butler moved toward the passenger seat and Sonia squeezed over his lap, her bottom rubbing against his thighs and genitals.

She got in the driver's seat, pressed the button, and stepped on the gas. The engine roared to life. She put down the emergency brake, turned on the lights, shifted into first, and they drove away.

"Head straight for the American Embassy," he said.

They took a left at the first intersection and found themselves on a wide tree-lined thoroughfare. There was little traffic and few pedestrians. The old stone buildings looked like apartment houses. Butler was surprised by the absence of stores and saloons, but this was the Soviet Union and there were fewer of them than in the West. They didn't have many stores because they didn't have much to sell, and the saloons closed early in an effort to curb alcoholism, which was a major social problem in the Soviet Union.

The sound of sirens was all around them, and seemed to be getting louder.

"I'll bet they're cordoning off the area of the city we're in," Sonia said, looking ahead out of the windshield. A streetlamp flashed on her finely chiseled features, and Butler thought how beautiful she was.

"Didn't you hear what I said?" she asked.

"I'm trying to think of what to do."

"Think fast, because once they cordon the area off, then they start to draw the net."

"Is the American Embassy in this neighborhood?"

"No, it's on the other side of the city near Red Square."

"Oh, shit."

"Stop swearing and tell me what to do!"

He looked at her, and her knuckles were white on the

steering wheel. Her hat was crooked on her head, and he wanted to straighten it.

"We've got to get out of this car and hide in one of these buildings," he said. "All the lights are out. Everybody must be asleep. Do you know anybody in this neighborhood?"

She gave him an evil look. "Are you kidding?"

"Why, what's wrong with this neighborhood?"

"This neighborhood has the reputation for having prostitutes."

"I didn't know they had prostitutes in Moscow."

"What are we going to do!"

The sirens were getting louder, and there was only one thing to do: abandon ship.

"Pull over to the curb right here," he said.

"Here?"

"That's right."

"Why here?"

"Because I said so."

"I think you want to find yourself a prostitute—that's why you want to stop here."

"Pull over and shut up."

She steered toward the curb, braked, and turned off the lights. "Now what?" she asked.

"Get out of the car."

"I can't turn the motor off."

"Open the hood, and I'll take care of that."

She pulled the latch and they got out of the car. He went under the hood and pulled apart his splice, causing the engine to stop. Then he slammed the hood shut.

"Let's go," he said. "Walk quickly and purposefully."

Side by side they marched down the street. At the corner they turned left, and at the next corner they turned right. The sound of sirens grew louder, and then they saw the headlights of a car turn the corner up ahead.

"Quick, down here!" he said.

He pushed her through a gateway and down some stairs to an entrance to the basement of a house. There was only a tiny corner in which to hide.

"Against here," he said, pushing her back to the wall. Then he squeezed against her.

The car came down the street slowly, its searchlight throwing a shaft of light over the sidewalks. Butler pressed harder against Sonia, hoping that the tiny niche would conceal them. He heard her breath against his ear and felt the outline of her body against his. The searchlight flashed past them, and he was getting an erection.

She began to squirm uncomfortably. "Stop that!" she snapped.

"I can't help it."

"Yes you can!"

"Ssshhhh."

"You're just trying to take advantage of me, you sex degenerate."

"You screw other women with a rubber dick, so who are you calling a sex degenerate?"

"I do not!"

"Then what do you do to them?"

"That's none of your business!"

"Not so loud."

"Let me out of here!"

"Wait until that car goes away."

"I SAID, LET ME..."

Butler clamped his hand over her mouth. She struggled, but she was a relatively dainty woman, while he was a relatively muscular man. He held her against the wall and chuckled as he rubbed his erection at her. Finally she stopped struggling and just leaned against the wall. He stopped moving too, and only squeezed against her gently.

"If you promise not to scream, I'll take my hand off your mouth."

She nodded her head, and he took his hand away.

"I think I'm going to throw up," she said.

"What a nasty little dyke you are."

"Dyke? What is a dyke?"

"It's American slang for a lesbian."

"Oh, shut up, you."

Butler drew his head back and looked into the street cautiously. He couldn't see the patrol car. Craning his head, he saw it turning the corner at the end of the street.

"We'd better get off the streets," Butler said. "Are you sure you don't know anybody in this neighborhood."

She gritted her teeth. "I told you already that I don't know anybody in this neighborhood. Only prostitutes and bums live in this neighborhood."

"Then it sounds like a good place for us, and this door right here is as good as any."

He took out his pick, bent over the lock, peered at it, and inserted the pick into the lock. Deftly he flicked over the tumblers, and then spun it around. It made a loud, snapping sound. He turned the knob and the door opened.

"In here," he told her.

They entered a dark vestibule that smelled moldy. He closed the door and locked it. Then he turned around, his eyes adjusting to the dimness. He could see a square of light in the distance, and pulled Sonia toward it. They shuffled down a long dank corridor, passed the furnace and hot water heater, and came to a door. The square of light was a window in the door, and they looked out into a courtyard. A big Zim sedan was parked there.

"I wonder what that car is doing here?" Sonia asked. "I don't think that the people in this neighborhood would have a car like that."

"How should I know what a car like that is doing here. My concern is that we can't stay here for long because at some point a janitor will come by to check the furnace and will see us. We've got to find a good place to hide."

"There are some stairs over there."

"Where?"

"There."

"Ah, I see them. Let's find out where they go. Follow me."

He led her up the stairs and at the top was a door. He tried the knob and it turned. Pushing gently, he opened the door and saw a carpeted corridor and papered walls.

"This looks like a classy joint," Butler said.

87

"It's a whorehouse, I tell you."

"It looks like an apartment building to me," he whispered. "I can see a door with a number on it."

"It's a whorehouse," she insisted.

"Your brain is a whorehouse, I think. Listen, I think our best bet is to hide in one of these apartments."

"Sure, so you can be with the whores."

"Follow me and do what I say. I'm going to open that door right there, and we're going into the apartment. Just keep your mouth shut when we go in and don't touch your gun.

I'll handle all the trouble if there happens to be any. Understand?"

"Why can't I use my gun too?"

"Because you'll probably shoot yourself or me by mistake."

"If I shoot you it won't be a mistake."

"If you don't stop talking to me that way I'm going to put my hand up your dress and pinch your behind."

"Don't you dare!"

"Ssshhhh."

He opened the door wider and they crept down the corridor. Butler sniffed for trouble and listened for ominous sounds. There was nothing. When he reached the door he had his pick ready. Slowly and silently he tickled the tumblers and turned them over. Then he twisted the knob gingerly. When it turned as far as it would go he pushed the door and peeked into a dark kitchen that glowed red in its far end.

"Come on," he whispered.

They tiptoed into the room and he closed the door silently. Immediately they became aware of three things: they were in a kitchen, a red light was on in a room adjacent to the kitchen, and from that room were issuing moans, sighs, and the sound of bedsprings creaking.

Butler brought his lips close to Sonia's ears. "I think somebody's fucking in there."

"I think so too."

"Come on—we'll take them by surprise."

"Oh, my goodness."

"You worry too much. Just stay close to me. Whatever you do, don't touch your gun, so I won't worry too much."

"I can't wait to see," she said, like a naughty little girl.

"Sssshhhh."

They tiptoed across the kitchen to the doorway and the red glow. The man was grunting and the woman was moaning. Butler and Sonia reached the doorway and peeked around it.

On a big bed two corpulent people were going at it like wild animals. The woman was on her back, kicking her pudgy legs in the air, and the man was pumping her. The sheets and blankets had fallen to the floor and the bed looked at though it would collapse any moment. Butler realized the two lovers were so preoccupied they wouldn't hear a bomb go off.

"I hate to break this up," he whispered to Sonia.

"Why don't you wait until they're finished," she replied.

"You're right, of course. It's the only decent thing to do."

So they peeked around the doorjamb and watched. Sonia was kneeling in front of him, and he was bending over her. The fat man took the woman's legs in his arms and socked it to her that way. She reached under him and cradled his testicles in her hand.

It was the raunchiest thing Butler ever saw in his life, though his own penis twitched to life. The fat man was groaning and farting, and the woman was screeching like a cat in heat. Butler looked down and saw Sonia's cute little bottom in front of him. He wanted to put his hand up her dress and feel it, but thought she might start to scream, the crazy dyke. But Butler was a red-blooded American man and he just couldn't stand there. So he gently rested his erection against the valley of her behind.

She stood bolt upright. "What do you think you're doing!" she demanded in a loud whisper.

Butler held his finger to his lips. "Not so loud."

"Did you just touch me!"

"As a matter of fact, I did."

"Don't you ever do that to me again!"

"Calm down."

"You're completely crazy and disgusting, do you know that?"

"You mean that's not turning you on in there?" He pointed to the fornicating twosome who were slobbering all over each other.

She shrugged. "A little."

"Oh, come on. Your tongue was practically hanging out."

"It was not!"

'It was too. Why don't you close your eyes and pretend that I'm a woman, and everything will be all right."

"Whatever can you be talking about?" she asked, shocked.

"Just turn around and watch, and make believe the most beautiful dyke in the world is behind you."

"You're sick, do you know that?"

"Yes, and so are you. Who do you think is the most beautiful woman in the world?"

"The French actress, Delphine Seyrig."

"My, what a kinky little thing you are. Turn around and watch the show."

He grabbed her shoulders and spun her around. The lady was on her hands and knees and the man was behind her, doing it doggie fashion. Sonia bent forward to see better, and Butler looked down at her fanny. He reached down and proceeded to caress it, but Sonia flinched at his touch.

"Pretend I'm Delphine," he whispered.

He expected her to turn around and slug him, but she didn't. She let him fondle her, and he figured she was so turned on by the *Satyricon* taking place in the bedroom that she was ready for anything. He lifted her dress and ran his fingers up her nylon thighs to her silky underpants. It was very damp there, and he realized that the girl was indeed quite horny. He slipped his fingers through the elastic leg band and touched her most delicate part, all covered with fleece. She trembled and he inserted his finger into the hot little cave. He went in deeper, his head spinning, his erection pounding in his pants.

Suddenly there was screaming and yelling from the vicinity of the bed. The fat man and fat lady were having an incredible coordinated orgasm. They clawed the air and each other, babbled and drooled, bounced around and jiggled. The bed looked like it might collapse and Butler wondered if the floor would hold out. Gradually their movements became less frenzied, and Butler realized that this monumental fuck was over. The time had come for him to make his move, if he wanted to have the element of surprise on his side.

He removed his finger from Sonia and moved his lips toward her ear. "When I snap my fingers, tell them to put their hands up and not to move, got it?"

"Yes."

Butler took out his pistol and pulled his visor down over his eyes so he'd look mean. The couple on the bed were lying exhausted in each other's arms, cooing like love birds.

Butler snapped his finger and charged into the room.

"Put your hands up!" Sonia screamed in Russian. "Don't move or we'll shoot!"

The man's head spun around. He had a thick black mustache and looked like a walrus. The woman's breath came in gasps.

"Oh, my goodness," Sonia said in Russian.

Butler didn't know what she said but could tell from the tone of her voice that something was wrong. "What is it?"

She stared at the man. "Don't you know who that is?"

Butler looked at him. The man had got out of bed and was standing naked and dripping with his hands in the air, a look of terror on his face. Butler had never seen him before in his life. "Who is he?"

"You don't know!"

"I told you that I don't."

"But that's... Vassily Streptakovich, the First Premier Deputy of the Communist Party!"

"Is he important?"

"He is the fifth most important man in all of Russia!"

Vassily Streptakovich smiled and bowed slightly. "Fourth," he said in English.

"Is that who you are?" Butler asked him.

Streptakovich wiggled his bushy eyebrows. "In all modesty, yes." His English sounded like it was coming from the bottom of a barrel of borscht, but Butler could understand him. "And this lady," Streptakovich continued, indicating with his hand the woman, "is Lizaveta Kartuzov, a dear friend of mine."

"So we've observed," Butler said.

"May I lower my hands?"

"By all means, do."

Streptakovich squared his shoulders and looked stern. "May I inquire what the KGB wants with me, a foremost leader of the Soviet state and a Hero of the People?"

Butler looked at Sonia, then returned his gaze to Streptakovich. "We're really not from the KGB."

"You're not?"

"No."

"Are you an American?"

"How did you guess?"

"I have visited your country many times. Beautiful place. I could tell from the way you speak that you are an American. Um, may I put some clothes on?"

"Not yet."

"But it's rather embarassing standing like this."

"It won't be for much longer."

"What are you doing in a KGB uniform? And who is she?"

"We have just escaped from your Kaluga Prison," Butler explained, "and now we're trying to get to the American Embassy. Perhaps you can help us?"

"Why were you in prison?"

"It's a long story. Anyway, since you're such a powerful

man in this country, maybe you can help us."

Streptakovich shook his head. "I'm afraid I couldn't do that. After all, a man of my position, you know how it is ..."

Butler pointed his pistol at him. "Either you help us, or you die."

Lizaveta Kartuzov put her fingers to her mouth and proceeded to cry.

Streptakovich looked sharply at her. "Quiet!"

She stopped crying.

Streptakovich looked at Butler. "What would you like me to do?"

"Is that your limousine downstairs?"

"As a matter of fact, it is. Nice car, eh?"

"Do you have a chauffeur?"

"He should be sleeping in the back seat."

"Good. I want you to take us to your office, and then I want you to arrange for Dr. Igor Kahlovka, who is a prisoner of the KGB, to be brought to your office. Then all of us will go in your car to the American Embassy. Once we all are safely inside, you may leave with Ms. Kartuzov. Is that clear?"

"Who is this Dr. Kahlovka?" Streptakovich asked.

"A Soviet scientist."

"What do you want with him?"

"None of your business. Put your clothes on and let's go, or get ready to die."

"My clothes are in the closet," Streptakovich said, pointing to it. "May I get them?"

"Move slowly." Butler looked at Ms. Kartuzov. "You put your clothes on too, because you're coming with us."

"May I turn on another light?"

"Go ahead."

She flicked on a lamp beside the bed, then walked on tiptoes to the closet, where Streptakovich was opening the door. He took out a suit on a hanger and placed it on the bed. "How long were you watching us?" he asked as he removed the clothes from the hanger.

"Quite some time."

"It was very kind of you not to interrupt us until we were finished."

"That would have been most inappropriate."

Streptakovich stepped into a pair of big baggy shorts. "You are a spy?"

"No, I'm a tourist."

"And her?" He motioned with his chin at Sonia.

"A friend of mine. Say, you don't know anything about that microwave machine that confuses smart bombs, do you?"

"What machine?" Streptakovich asked, but the expression on his face gave him away. He knew.

"A microwave machine—it makes smart bombs inaccurate."

Streptakovich shrugged as he put on his shirt. "Where did you hear about that?"

"People talk."

"Not to me, unfortunately. But when a man reaches my high station in life, people are afraid to tell you things. But I know that you are a spy. You have CIA written all over you. Who did you say told you about the microwave machine?"

"I'll ask the questions." Butler jiggled his gun significantly.

Lizaveta Kartuzov was rummaging in the closet. "Should I wear my brown dress or my gray dress?" she asked Streptakovich in Russian.

"What the hell so I care?" he replied.

While Streptakovich and Lizaveta were dressing, Butler walked to Sonia's side. Her arms were crossed under her bulging boobs and she looked distraught as usual.

"How do you feel?" he asked.

"We'll never make it," she replied.

"You have no faith in me."

"Why should I have faith in you?"

"I got you out of prison, didn't I?"

"You're also the one who got me *into* prison."

"Natalia got both of us in prison, but this is no time to quibble. Soon we'll leave for this man's office, and after we

94

get the good Dr. Kahlovka, we head for the American Embassy. You'll be in the United States before you know it, watching television in some dyke bar someplace."

"Easier said than done."

"We'll do it."

"Don't be so sure. Do you know where his office is?"

"No. Where is it?"

"The Kremlin."

Butler flinched. "The Kremlin?"

"That's right, and if you think you're going to buzz in and out of there like it's some kind of train station, you're crazy."

The Kremlin? Butler thought, turning from Sonia. How the hell am I going to pull this one off?

12

They walked toward the corridor to the back door of the building. Streptakovich wore a black coat and fur hat, while Lizaveta wore a brown coat and no hat, her long blonde hair spilling over her collar. Butler and Sonia had straightened their uniforms and wore their hats low over their faces.

"Don't forget," Butler said to Streptakovich. "Do anything foolish, and I'll shoot you."

"I'll cooperate as best I can. Just don't be too trigger crazy, if you know what I mean."

"Just don't do anything that might make me think you're trying to signal somebody that we're holding you hostage."

"Please calm down. By the way, what did you say your name was?"

"I didn't say."

They went out the back door and descended a short flight of stairs to the courtyard, where the big Zim limousine sat in the driveway. They approached the car and Streptakovich knocked on the back window. A figure inside jumped up, and the door opened.

"Ah, Comrade Streptakovich," the chauffeur said sleepily. He was no older than nineteen and had pimples on his thin, sallow face. He looked at his watch, then at Lizaveta and the strange couple in the KGB uniforms. It was easy to see that he was confused.

"Take me to my office," Streptakovich growled.

"Yes, comrade."

Streptakovich sat in back between Butler and Sonia, while Lizaveta took the front seat beside the driver, who started up the limousine, turned on the lights, and drove out of the courtyard. When he reached the street he turned left.

The limousine passed through the city of Moscow. The sky was black-streaked with reddish clouds, and against them was the weird skyline of cupolas and balisks. There was little traffic; it was three o'clock in the morning and the city was sleeping.

"Have you heard the news?" the driver asked in Russian.

"What news?" Streptakovich asked.

"Some prisoners have escaped from the Kaluga Prison. They killed a few of the guards."

"You don't say."

Streptakovich looked at Butler and Sonia. He was starting to get the picture. Finally the limousine entered Red Square. At one end was Saint Basil's Cathedral, at the other end was Lenin's Tomb, and on the side was the Kremlin. The buildings were all lit up, and Butler knew that somewhere in the area was the U.S. Embassy. He was tempted to go there immediately, but his original mission was to get Dr. Kahlovka out of the Soviet Union, and by God that's what he was going to do. The danger of the situation didn't especially intimidate Butler. He'd been in dangerous situations before. He had a cool head and a steady trigger finger.

They approached the Kremlin, and Butler was surprised by how much it resembled the Kaluga Prison. There was the same high wall surrounding stone buildings inside. The limousine rolled toward the gate, and the guards recognized the vehicle. They opened the gates and saluted it as it went past them.

The car rumbled over the cobblestones within the Kremlin. Butler looked at the buildings and could see lights on in some of the buildings. He imagined Lenin and Stalin swaggering along the sidewalks, and the Czars before them.

The limousine stopped in front of one of the stone buildings. It was five stories high and looked like it had been built sometime in the last century by the same architect who had designed the palace at Versailles. It managed to look solid and ornate at the same time.

"Tell the driver to wait here," Butler said to Streptakovich.

Streptakovich gave the instructions to the driver, then they left the car and entered the building. They walked down a long corridor covered with red carpet, and on the walls were oil paintings of heroes of the Revolution. Finally they came to a wooden door, and Streptakovich opened it. They entered the wood-paneled office area where Streptakovich's secretaries worked during the day, and then passed on to Streptakovich's office.

Streptakovich snapped on a lamp on his desk. It revealed a large wood-paneled office with a painting of Lenin behind the desk and a painting of Streptakovich himself as a young man in a military uniform on the opposite wall. Two Soviet flags on short flagpoles were on either side of Lenin's portrait.

"May I take off my coat?" Streptakovich asked.

"Go ahead."

Streptakovich hung his coat in the closet, and then took Lizaveta's and hung it up too. He walked to the chair behind his desk and sat down, rubbing his hands. "What now?" he asked.

"Get us Dr. Kahlovka."

"That might take a while."

Butler took out his pistol and pointed it at Streptakovich's head. "It'd better not." Then he looked at Sonia. "Pick up the extension over there," he pointed to a phone on a wooden table, "and listen to what he says. If he so much as suggests that we're here, tell me and I'll blow his brains out."

Streptakovich shook his head. "That will not be necessary, I assure you."

"I don't trust you as far as I can throw you, Streptakovich,

98

and you weigh at least three hundred pounds."

Streptakovich picked up the telephone, thought for a few seconds, then hung it up again. "I don't know what to say," he confessed.

"Just call whoever you were going to call and tell them to bring Dr. Kahlovka here immediately. Say that some KGB agents have uncovered new information about his activities, and you want to question him personally."

"But that would be most irregular."

"You're the number four man in the Soviet Union, Streptakovich. You don't have to take any shit from anybody."

Streptakovich nodded. "That's true." He picked up the phone, dialed a number, and after a while began to talk. Sonia listened on the other phone while he spoke to the commandant of the Kaluga Prison and demanded that Dr. Kahlovka be brought to him immediately.

"But what on earth for?" asked the commandant on the other end of the phone.

"You dare ask me why I do things? Don't you know who I am?" Streptakovich thundered.

"Yes, comrade. I'm sorry, comrade. I'll have him delivered to your office immediately and without delay, comrade."

"See that you do," Streptakovich snarled, hanging up the phone. Then he looked at Butler. "I did it."

"I guess now we have to wait. You got any cigarettes?"

"No, but I have some fine Cuban cigars."

"I'll have one, if you don't mind."

"I don't mind at all."

Sonia stood up. "I'll have one too."

Butler looked at her.

Streptakovich looked at Butler.

"Let her have one," Butler said.

Streptakovich, Butler, and Sonia took cigars and Streptakovich lit them with a lighter he had on his desk. It was in the shape of a metal cube and had an embossed bust of Marx on one side, and a bust of Lenin on the opposite side.

"I'm bored," said Lizaveta, fanning her mouth.

"Who cares?" Streptakovich said.

Lizaveta frowned and leaned back in the chair. Sonia stood at the window and looked out, while Butler paced the floor, trying to figure out what his options were. The hand moved slowly around the clock on the wall. Butler realized he didn't have many options. All he could do was try to make it to the embassy with Sonia and Dr. Kahlovka. He walked to Sonia, who was puffing her cigar.

"How're you doing?" he asked.

"I'm contemplating death," she replied.

"Good grief."

"I've decided that it might be a wonderful escape from this horrible humdrum life."

"But when you escape, you usually go from one thing to another. When you die, you go from one thing to nothing."

"I think that's what I can use right now. Nothing."

"You Russians are so melancholy."

"And you Americans are so adolescent."

"It's adolescent to want to live?"

"You're just a very silly man."

"I want to live because I have something to live for."

"What's that?"

"I want to make love to you."

"What!"

"You heard me."

"Forget about it, idiot."

"I touched you in Lizaveta's apartment, and now I want to have you."

"You'll never have me."

"Didn't you like it when I touched you? It felt as though you liked it."

"You were not touching me—Delphine Seyrig was touching me."

"You know very well it was me."

"If I thought it was you I would have thrown up."

Butler walked away from her. Streptakovich sat at his desk, puffing the cigar and drumming his fingers. Lizaveta looked at her nails.

"I hope my wife doesn't find out about this," Streptakovich said.

"You mean Lizaveta's not your wife?" Butler asked.

"Of course not. She is my mistress. Every major communist leader has a mistress. After all, who do you think we are? We are not a backward people."

"Oh," Butler said.

"But I love Lizaveta," Streptakovich continued. "There's going to be a terrible scandal when all this is over."

"Why don't you defect to the West?" Butler asked.

"Defect?"

"Sure."

Streptakovich scratched his chin. "I never thought of that."

"Why don't you think about it now."

"Hmmmm," Streptakovich said. "Hmmmmmmmm." He looked at Butler. "Do you think I could get a job in America?"

"Sure. The government probably will find a job for you to repay you for defecting."

"I have always wanted to own a restaurant," Streptakovich said dreamily.

"Oh, it's easy to own a restaurant in America. The government probably will lend you the money."

"And maybe I could play a balalaika, and stroll among the diners."

"Sounds terrific. And Lizaveta will be one of your waitresses."

"Yes. That would be marvelous."

"And you know there's no future for you here. You're liable to get purged any moment."

"Especially after this incident."

"How true."

Butler rested his fists on Streptakovich's desk and leaned toward him. "Come with us. There's a brave new world waiting for you in America."

"I don't know—I'll have to think about it."

"You don't have much time, Streptakovich."

He gritted his teeth. "I know, I know."

There was a knock on the door. Everybody sprang to their feet. Butler looked at Streptakovich. "Get the prisoner and dismiss the people who brought him. Don't do anything strange. Otherwise I'll have to shoot you, and I'd hate to do that in view of the warm relationship that has grown between us during the past two hours."

"I quite understand," Streptakovich said.

Streptakovich walked to the door with Sonia and Butler on either side of him. He opened the door and there were four KGB guards with a bedraggled individual who Butler figured was Dr. Kahlovka. The KGB guards all saluted Streptakovich, who looked at Kahlovka and sniffed.

"I'll handle him now," Streptakovich said in Russian. "You may return to your posts."

"Yes, comrade," the guards said in unison. They saluted, did an about-face, and marched away.

"Into my office!" Streptakovich ordered Dr. Kahlovka.

Like a frightened squirrel, Dr. Kahlovka skittered into the office. Butler shut the door and bolted it. Dr. Kahlovka wore baggy pants, an overcoat too large for him, and no shoes. He had a Lenin-style beard, his hair was mussed, and he looked like hell as he peered fearfully into the faces of Butler, Sonia, Streptakovich, and Lizaveta.

"Do you speak English?" Butler asked.

"Yes," Kahlovka replied fearfully.

Butler smiled and held out his hand. "I'm Butler from the Institute. I missed you on the beach near Tallinn a fortnight ago, but you were unavoidably detained, I understand. Anyway, here I am again, and we're going to the American Embassy right away. Don't tell them anything there; save it for your debriefing at the Institute."

Dr. Kahlovka looked as though his eyeballs would fall out of his head. "Where did you get the KGB uniform?" he stammered.

"That's a long story."

"How did you get in here?"

"That's a longer story."

Kahlovka's trembling finger pointed at Streptakovich.

"Isn't that the First Premier Deputy of the Communist Party?"

"It is."

"Is he in the Institute too?"

"No."

"Then what's he doing here?"

"This is his office. It's exactly where he should be. But he is cooperating for one reason." Butler took out his pistol and twirled it around his finger.

"I see," said Kahlovka.

Butler looked him in the eye. "We're going to make a break for the U.S. Embassy right now. It's possible that all of us might not make it. That young woman over there is Sonia Barsovina, also a member of the Institute. You'd better tell us all you know about the microwave machine right now, because if you don't make it, the Institute won't be able to stop the terror that's threatening to engulf the world."

Dr. Kahlovka raised his fingers in the air and wiggled them. "I don't have the plans for how it's made, but before I was arrested by the KGB I found out that they're building it not in the Vasilkov Munitions Plant in Moscow as we previously thought, but in the Abdul Faheem Munitions Plant in Syria."

"Syria?" Butler asked.

"Yes."

"Why Syria?"

"Because the Russian generals want Syria to attack Israel with the new weapons and utterly vanquish her. The Americans, of course, will intervene, and that will give the Russians an excuse to intervene. The Russian generals hope to defeat the American Army in Israel, insist on unconditional surrender, then win all of America in the spoils of war, and get all the factories and cities intact. They figure that will be smarter than attacking the American mainland directly because the wealth of America would be destroyed."

"When is all this supposed to happen?"

"A few weeks."

Butler looked at Streptakovich. "Is that right?"

Streptakovich nodded sadly. "I believe it is."

"But it's crazy!"

Streptakovich shrugged. "There are a lot of fanatics in this country who are hungry to go to war. They control the government."

Butler frowned. "There are a lot of the same kind of people in our country too."

Streptakovich looked at the ceiling. "If there was only some kind of organization that was trying to put an end to all this madness."

Butler grabbed him by the shoulder. "If there was, would you join it?"

"Of course. I want peace to come to the world so I can have a little restaurant someplace, where I can play my balalaika, and Lizaveta could welcome the guests."

"There is such an organization, Streptakovich. Defect, and you can join it."

"There couldn't be such an organization!"

"There is, and it could use you. Will you join us?"

"I don't know. I'd have to give it very careful consideration."

"You don't have time for careful consideration, Streptakovich. The shit is about to hit the fan. You've got to decide *now*.

Streptakovich put his hand to his forehead. "I can't think under pressure!" He looked at Lizaveta. "Should we go?"

"Will I be able to live in New York City and buy my clothes at Saks Fifth Avenue?"

Streptakovich turned to Butler. "Will she?"

"Why not?"

Lizaveta clasped her hands together. "Then let's go, Vassily!"

Streptakovich scratched his head. "I don't know. I'd have to give up all this." With a wave of his hand he indicated his office.

"We've got to get out of here," Butler said. "Streptakovich, you lead the way."

They got their coats out of the closet and put them on. Then Streptakovich opened the door to his office and led them down the corridor. Butler looked at his watch—it was five o'clock in the morning. They passed under portraits of revolutionary heroes still in favor with the regime, and then rounded a corner. They saw coming toward them a man in a suit, smoking a cigarette and carrying a briefcase stuffed full of papers. As this man approached, Butler recognized his portliness and gorilla features as belonging to none other than the Number One Man in the Soviet Union, Leonid Brezhnev!

"Good morning Comrade Brezhnev," said Streptakovich with a slight bow.

"Good morning, Comrade Streptakovich," Brezhnev replied, looking curiously at the entourage following Streptakovich. He wrinkled his massive brow at the sight of Doctor Kahlovka in raggedy clothes and no shoes.

But the group of people continued walking purposefully. Butler expected Brezhnev to call for the guards at any moment and thought he might have to shoot the sonofabitch if that happened, but they came to the door and were out of the building without incident.

It was still dark and there was not even a suggestion of dawn. They walked across the cobblestones to Streptakovich's limousine, and the driver was sleeping in the back seat as usual. Streptakovich woke him up, and the strange group piled into the car. Streptakovich sat in back with Sonia and Butler on either side of him, and in front with the driver were Lizaveta and Dr. Kahlovka.

"Drive to the United States Embassy," Streptakovich told the driver.

"The United States Embassy?" the driver asked, astonished.

"Do as I say!"

"Yes, comrade."

The limousine rolled over the narrow passageways inside the Kremlin. Butler thought of Ivan the Terrible and Czar

Nicholas II and the great tumultuous history of Russia. And here he was at the seat of power himself. He felt as though he were trapped inside a history book.

Streptakovich cleared his throat. "What if the people at the U.S. Embassy don't let you in?" he asked Butler.

"They'll let us in. The Marines on duty at all U.S. embassies are instructed to let through possible defectors, and that's us."

"Maybe not," said Streptakovich.

"You're not coming with us?"

"I don't think so. My first loyalty must be to Mother Russia."

"They're going to string you up by your toes when all this is over, Streptakovich. Remember the fate of Leon Trotsky."

Streptakovich shook his head. "I don't know what to do."

"You don't have much time to make up your mind."

"I detest making decisions under pressure."

They came to the front gate of the Kremlin and the guards opened it up, saluting the car. They passed through the gate and entered Red Square. Already at that time of the morning a huge line had gathered in front of Lenin's Tomb to see the preserved body of Vladimir Ilyich Lenin, the leader of the Communist Revolution. The driver steered across Red Square, the only vehicle upon it that time of the morning.

And then in the distance they heard the sound of sirens. Butler spun his head around. A herd of cars with spinning red lights on top screeched around the corner of the Kremlin and appeared to be coming after the car in which Butler was sitting.

"Uh-oh," said Butler. "They're on to us!"

"Oh no!" cried Streptakovich.

Sonia leaned forward and stuck her pistol into the driver's ear. "Drive to the American Embassy as quickly as you can, understand?"

"Yes, comrade."

The driver stomped down on his accelerator, and the limousine leapt ahead like a tiger. It gathered speed and zoomed across Red Square, heading straight for the long line of people who'd come to see Lenin's corpse. The people saw the car coming, realized it had no intention of stopping or slowing down, and scattered out of its way like barnyard chickens. Butler looked out the rear window and saw that there were six cars in pursuit, sirens wailing and red lights spinning on their roofs. There was the sound of a shot, and a bullet crashed into the trunk of the car.

"Everybody get down!" Butler said.

They all ducked except the driver, Butler, and Sonia, who kept her pistol stuck in the driver's ear. Butler rolled down the rear window, turned around, stuck his pistol out, and fired at the pursuing vehicles. The buildings surrounding Red Square echoed with the reports of the guns. Butler gritted his teeth and fired round after round at the pursuing cars, realizing that this would be making page one of every newspaper in the world in a few hours. A bullet found its mark in the left rear tire of the car and the tire exploded, sending the car careening out of control. But the driver struggled with the wheel and brought the car under control again. He had made it across Red Square and zipped into Gorky Street, on which the United States Embassy was located.

It was a gray stone building like the other buildings in the area, and it was surrounded by a steel fence. Two marine guards were in front looking at the advancing cars and then at each other. They realized that one car was being pursued by six, and that maybe the one car contained defectors. They called for help on their walkie-talkie and then opened the gates.

"Drive right in!" Sonia told the driver, nudging his ear with her pistol.

"Yes, comrade."

He spun the wheel to the right, the car turned and screeched, and shot into the compound of the United States Embassy. The Marine guards closed the gates and other Marines came running in all directions.

"Into the building!" Butler yelled, throwing open his door.

The six KGB cars roared to a halt in front of the Embassy gates, their headlights shining on Butler, Sonia, and Dr. Kahlovka running toward the door of the Embassy being held open by a marine.

Butler looked back as he ascended the stairs. "Come on, Streptakovich!"

Streptakovich sat in the car, chewing his fingernails. "I can't make up my mind," he whined.

"I can make up mine," Lizaveta replied, "and I'm going!" She jumped out of the car and headed for the steps.

"But Lizaveta!"

She didn't hear him; her head was spinning with dreams of fashions from Saks Fifth Avenue.

"I think I'm going to go too," said the driver, pushing open his door.

"But comrade..."

"Up your ass, Streptakovich." The driver got out of the car and ran up the stairs of the Embassy.

Streptakovich sat alone in the back seat of his limousine. He looked out the rear window and saw the KGB agents arguing with U.S. Marines. It appeared to be the type of situation that could set off an international incident. He tried to imagine what would happen to him if he didn't defect, and remembered what happened to the soldiers who surrendered to the Germans during World War Two. When they were repatriated, they were sent to the slave camps in Siberia, and Streptakovich didn't want that fate to befall him. I have no choice, he thought. The Americans probably will treat me better than my own people.

That made up his mind. He dived out the door of the car and began waddling toward the steps of the embassy.

"Comrade Streptakovich, where are you going!" shouted one of the KGB agents in front of the gate.

"To Disneyland!" Streptakovich yelled over his shoulder as he climbed the stairs.

108

13

Each of the defectors was put in a separate room with no windows and a guard at the door. Butler's room was a small sitting room with two sofas facing each other and a number of chairs sprinkled throughout the room. On the wall hung a portrait of George Washington, and Butler stretched out on the sofa, his hands behind his head. He was safe. He'd done it again. And now he'd have to get to the nearest office of the Institute as quickly as he could to relay the latest information on the Doom Machine.

The door of the office opened and in walked a man of forty-five wearing a blue Brooks Brothers suit with white shirt and red tie. His bald pate had freckles on it, he had a nose like a button, and he looked as though he played tennis every day.

"Hi there," he said, extending his hand to Butler.

"Hello." Butler stood and shook his hand.

"No—don't get up—that's all right." The man pulled up a chair and sat beside the sofa that Butler was using. "My name's Hardy, Alfred Hardy, and I'm one of the assistants to the Ambassador."

Butler smiled politely, but he knew this guy was from the CIA. Who else would want to interview a bunch of people who crashed through the gates of the Embassy?

"Rather exciting thing you just did, what?" Hardy said.

"Yes," Butler agreed.

"Would you mind telling me your name?"

"Not at all. It's Butler."

"You have your passport with you?"

"Afraid not." Butler patted the pockets of his KGB uniform. "This isn't mine."

"Can you tell me in your own words what has happened, Mr. Butler?"

"Well, I was in the Soviet Union on business, and for some reason the KGB picked me up and threw me in prison. I escaped with a few other people, managed to hi-jack a car, and made it over here."

"That's incredible!" said Hardy.

"But true," replied Butler.

"What were you doing in the Soviet Union in the first place?"

"I was sent here by my company, the Bancroft Research Institute, to do some business with the Russians, but before I knew what hit me, I was arrested and put in prison."

"You don't know why?"

"Not at all."

"Hmmmm. And did you ever see any of the other people before?"

"No."

"Do you know who they are?"

"The guy who owned the car is evidently pretty high up in the Soviet government."

"Hmmmm. I see. Would you excuse me for a moment, Mr. Butler?"

"Sure."

"Oh, by the way, could you give me your social security number?"

Butler did.

"Thank you. See you in a little while." Hardy bounded out of his chair and headed for the door.

"Have you got a cigarette on you by any chance?" Butler asked.

"As a matter of fact, I do."

Hardy spun around, returned to Butler, took out a pack of Marlboros, and gave him one. He lit it, then left the room.

Butler crossed his legs on the sofa and puffed the cigarette. He knew that Hardy would run his name and social security number through the computer and find out that Butler was an ex-CIA man with a strange past. He wondered what was going on outside the Embassy, and could imagine the frantic phone calls between the Kremlin and Washington. The Kremlin would insist on keeping everybody within the Soviet Union, and the United States would insist on bringing everybody out.

Presently Hardy returned to the room, a handful of paper in his hand and a frown on his face. He sat opposite Butler and looked him in the eye. "You were in the CIA, weren't you Butler?"

"Yes, I was."

"Oh, that's going to make things very sticky, Butler. The Soviets already are claiming that you are all CIA agents, and they don't even know the truth yet. What a stink they'll raise. They'll probably take it all the way to the floor of the United Nations. Um, you're not still working for us are you?"

"No."

"What did you say you were doing in the Soviet Union?"

"I was here on business."

"What kind of business."

"Looking for an office. My company was planning to open a branch here."

"Hmmm. And you never saw any of those other people before?"

"No sir."

"Hmmmm."

14

Negotiations continued at the highest levels of the Soviet and American government while newspapers throughout the world told the story of the six who were being held incommunicado in the U.S. Embassy in Moscow. Left wing newspapers said they were CIA agents and it was all a big CIA plot to undermine the workers' paradise, while right wing newspapers claimed they were freedom fighters and advocates of private enterprise. As usual, the public didn't get the truth because the newspapers didn't know what the truth was, and even if they did, they would have distorted it to fit their ideological point of view.

Finally the Secretary General of the United Nations flew to Moscow and held direct talks with the leaders of the Soviet government. After much lying and haranguing, it was finally agreed to exchange the "Moscow Six," as they came to be called, for Soviet KGB agents languishing in various prisons throughout the world.

At one o'clock on a Wednesday morning, the Moscow Six boarded a bus in the back of the U.S. Embassy in Moscow. It was the first time they'd seen each other since their daring escape across Red Square. They greeted each other politely but didn't say much of consequence because they knew the bus must be wired for sound. They were driven from the embassy to Moscow International Airport, where they boarded a U.S. Air Force jet transport plane bound for Washington D.C.

Butler sat with Sonia, Streptakovich sat with Lizaveta, and Doctor Kahlovka sat with the chauffeur. Butler, Sonia, and Doctor Kahlovka had been given American-style clothes to wear, and Butler had shaved the night before, splashing on a little Aqua Velva on afterwards. The six buckled themselves into their seats, while various CIA and embassy people occupied other seats. The plane raced down the runway and leapt into the sky.

They were out of the Soviet Union and bound for the United States at last.

Butler leaned toward Sonia and whispered, "They treat you all right?"

"Very well, thank you," she said with a smile.

"You're happy?"

"Very happy, and I owe it all to you."

"You also owe me a hundred rubles. Remember our bet?"

"I remember. You know, you're not bad-looking at all, now that I can see your face."

"Do I look as good as Delphine Seyrig?"

"You never could look that good. And you're not going to win that other hundred rubles either."

"Oh yes I am."

"Oh no you're not."

The plane landed at Heathrow Airport outside London for refueling and then continued across the Atlantic Ocean to Washington D.C. It landed at ten o'clock in the evening at Dulles International Airport and a huge crowd was waiting to catch a glimpse of the celebrities. A battalion of police was on hand to keep the people back, and photographers began to take pictures as soon as the doors of the airplane opened.

The Moscow Six walked down the steps to the runway, where microphones were set up. The Vice-President of the United States greeted them along with various State Department officials and congresspersons trying to get into the act. Several of them made speeches in which they spoke of such subjects as freedom and justice, and then the

113

members of the Moscow Six were invited to say something to the crowds.

The microphones were hooked up to loudspeakers as well as radio stations in America and throughout the world. They also were being used by various television stations who had camera crews doing on-the-spot coverage.

Streptakovich was the first to use the microphones. "It is wonderful for me to be in this great country," he said happily. "Thank you very much."

Sonia was next and she said she was overjoyed to be in America.

Lizaveta wrung her hands and cried and said thank you in Russian which nobody understood.

The chauffeur asked if anybody knew where he could get a job, but he said it in Russian and nobody understood him either.

Doctor Kahlovka said that he was looking forward to enjoying the freedom that Americans are supposed to have.

Butler said it was good to be home.

Amid cheering crowds and flashbulbs popping all around them, they were escorted to a waiting bus that drove them to the CIA headquarters in Langley, Virginia.

15

"Now see here, Butler, just what the hell is going on here!" said F.J. Shankham, director of the Office of Current Intelligence of the CIA. A lean, sallow man, Shankham once had been Butler's superior in the New York counterintelligence station.

"I already told the other people, Shankham. How many times do I have to go through it?"

"Till I'm satisfied you're telling the truth." Shankham looked down his long thin nose at Butler. They were sitting in Shankham's office in CIA headquarters. "You don't expect me to believe you really were in Moscow just to rent office space, do you?"

"That's what I was doing there. Call my boss at the Bancroft Institute if you don't believe me."

"Already spoke to him. He confirmed your story, but I still think there's something fishy. The Russians insist you and the Barsovina woman were spying on them, and I wouldn't be surprised if they were right. The question is: who are you spying for? I know it's not the Bancroft Institute—they're a completely above-board scientific organization as far as we know, but I think you're just using them as the cover for something else. Who are you working for on the side, Butler? The Army? The Navy? The Air Force? A foreign power?"

"Your imagination is running away with you as usual, Shankham. I'm just an ordinary working stiff these days. Just trying to make an honest living. Unlike you."

Shankham widened his eyes. "What do you mean, unlike me? Are you taking another of your cheap potshots at the CIA, Butler?"

"Who me?"

"Yes, you. You always were bad-mouthing us even when you worked for us. I used to wonder why you joined us in the first place."

"I was young and idealistic. I didn't realize that the CIA spends most of its time and budget subverting the governments of countries it doesn't like. How much of the taxpayers' money did you spend to bring down Allende? Twenty million dollars?"

Shankham looked at the ceiling. "There you go, yapping about Allende again. You never change, Butler. You're like a broken record."

"But I did change. I got out of the CIA. You're the one who's still here."

"You're damn right I'm still here. And I'm going to be here until I drop."

"You're the broken record, not me. All I was trying to do was fix the broken record, and the CIA fired me."

Shankham frowned. "But it was so depressing having you around, Butler. You were always complaining. Your problem is that you were soft on Communism."

"Your problem is that you're soft in the head."

"Now hold on there, Butler. Let's not make this personal."

Butler leaned forward in his chair. "I want to get out of here, Shankham. I'm an American citizen and you've got no right to hold me. I'm going to get a lawyer and sue you bastards if you don't turn me loose."

"Why don't you tell us what you were really doing in the Soviet Union, Butler. Why must you be so difficult?"

"I'm not being difficult. I already told you what I was doing there."

"I mean the truth."

"That's the truth."

Shankham held out the palms of his hands. "Why don't you cooperate with your government?" he pleaded. "Is it so hard for you to cooperate with your government?"

"In the first place, I have cooperated, and in the second place, the government belongs to the billionaire industrial multinational class, not me. I'm just another poor working stiff."

Shankham closed his eyes and shook his head. "Oh, Butler, you're so tiresome."

"Then why don't you let me go?"

"I will. You're dismissed. Get the fuck out of here before I take my gun out of my desk and shoot you."

"Now, now," Butler cooed, standing up. "Let's not let our temper get the best of us."

"You make me mad, Butler. You're so full of shit."

Butler headed toward the door. "See you around, Shankham. Take it easy."

"You're the one who'd better take it easy," Shankham growled.

16

A CIA chauffeur drove Butler to the office of the Bancroft Research Institute in Georgetown, a three-story brownstone on a quiet tree-shaded street. Butler entered the building and approached the receptionist at the front desk, but before he could say anything she looked at him and exclaimed, "You're Butler, aren't you?"

"Yes, ma'am."

"We've been expecting you. Mr. Sheffield is here. Just wait a second and I'll buzz him."

She pressed a button on her desk and mumbled into her telephone. Then she hung it up and looked at Butler again. "He's in room 316—know where it is?"

"Yes, ma'am."

Butler climbed the winding spiral staircase to the third floor and knocked on the door marked 316.

"Come in," said the familiar voice of Mr. Sheffield.

Butler entered the room and closed the door. It was dark and Sheffield sat behind a desk, spotlights illuminating the papers before him.

"Good to see you again, Butler," Sheffield said. "I understand things got a little tight in the Soviet Union."

"They sure did."

"Well have a seat, and tell me about it."

Butler sat in a chair before the desk, and a spotlight in the ceiling came on to bathe him in golden light.

"To begin with," Butler said, "that Natalia girl was a KGB agent."

"You don't say."

"I do say. She nearly got me and everybody else killed. Somehow she beat your lie-detector machines."

"That's certainly not good news. Let me make a note of it." Sheffield wrote something on a piece of paper. "Whatever became of her?" Sheffield said, looking up.

"I killed her."

"I see."

"It was necessary."

"I should hope so. Did you find out anything about the Doom Machine?"

"Yes, I spoke to Doctor Kahlovka briefly before we went to the U.S. Embassy in Moscow. He told me that the Russians are having the Doom Machine built at the Abdul Faheem Munitions Plant in Damascus. The plan is that the Syrians will attack Israel and demolish her. The Americans will enter the war to save the pieces, then Russia will send their troops in with more Doom Machines. The Third World War will then take place with the Middle East as the locale, and the Russians will win because they have the Doom Machine. The Americans will surrender at one point, and the Russians will rule the world. They will occupy America, which will be intact, and plunder it. The end."

"Hmmm," said Sheffield. "They want to fight the war on a battlefield where nothing of strategic importance can be damaged."

"Exactly."

"But they're forgetting one thing."

"What's that?"

"That the Israelis have the atomic bomb."

"I didn't know that."

"You know it now. If the Israelis ever are hard-pressed, you can be sure they'll use it, and you probably can guess what their first target will be."

"Damascus?"

"You're close, but guess again."

"Moscow?"

"They never could deliver a warhead to Moscow. No, they'd drop it right on the oil fields of Saudi Arabia and make the biggest bonfire the world has ever seen."

"It'll probably burn up the whole Middle East and everything in it."

"It might even be worse than that. That oil, don't forget, is deep in the ground. If it's ignited with an atomic weapon, the explosion might very well split this entire planet right down the middle."

"What!"

"It's true. That much of an explosion deep in the ground could destroy our planet."

"We've got to tell the Russians!"

"Their own scientists probably have told them, but they won't listen. Military fanatics can't see anything except their dream of victory. No, we've got to handle this ourselves, and we don't have much time. I know you've just been on two difficult operations in a row, and you deserve a rest, but I wonder if we could count on you to stay on this with us. We'll need someone to go into action right away, and I don't think we'll have much time to brief someone new."

"Of course you can count on me, sir."

"Good man." Sheffield looked at his watch. "It's three o'clock in the afternoon. I'll have to meet with the Executive Council on this, so why don't you report back to my office here at nine o'clock in the morning? That'll give you a few hours to unwind. By the way, where are you staying?"

"I'm not staying anywhere yet."

"Then why don't you stay at the Albemarle Hotel? We maintain a suite of rooms there for our travelling personnel, and it's a most distinguished residence. I'm sure you'll like it."

"I'm sure I will too, since you recommend it so highly."

Mister Sheffield chortled. "Why, thank you, Butler. And by the way, we have a number of vehicles assigned to our office here. You can take one of them if you like."

"I think it would be easier to take cabs." Butler stood up. "Is that all, sir?"

"Yes, until tomorrow morning at nine."

"See you then," Butler said with a wave, turning toward the door.

17

Butler went down to the basement, where the wardrobe room was located, and selected a brown tweed suit of conservative cut to replace the suit the Embassy had given him. He changed into the suit and matching accessories, then left the Institute office and wandered through the streets of Georgetown for fifteen minutes until he found a cab to take him to the Albemarle Hotel.

The hotel was in downtown Washington D.C., so Butler leaned back in the seat of the cab and tried to relax. The problem was that it usually took him three or four days to unwind, and he only had around sixteen hours until he had to work again. That meant he'd be tense all that time and probably not sleep much tonight. It'd be better if he could begin his next operation immediately, but Sheffield needed time to put together a plan.

The cab pulled up in front of the Albemarle Hotel, a sedate old brick building not far from Warren G. Harding Square. Butler paid the cabdriver, got out of the cab, and walked into the hotel's lobby, a vast wood-paneled area with paintings on the walls, a maroon rug on the floor, and chandeliers hanging from the ceiling. Gentlemen and ladies sat around on antique furniture chatting with each other or reading *The Wall Street Journal*. Butler walked to the check-in desk, identified himself, and asked for a key to one of the suites rented by the Institute. The clerk called the Institute to verify Butler's identity, then gave him the key and a big smile, for the clerk was gay. Butler took the key, turned, and walked toward the elevator.

"Is that you, Butler?"

Butler turned in the direction of the familiar female voice and found himself staring into the beautiful face of Brenda Day, his first wife.

"Well," Butler said, his heart faltering, "if it isn't my dearly beloved wife number one."

"It is you, isn't it Butler?" She peered into his eyes, and hers were blue as a Magritte sky. Her hair was golden and if you saw her you might think she was the young woman who had won the Miss America contest several years ago. She wore a black mouton coat and a matching black mouton hat cocked to the side of her head.

"It is I, my dear," he said.

Her blue eyes roved over his face. "Still as handsome and dashing as ever, I see."

"What a kind thing to say to the catastrophe I have become."

She patted her palm on his chest. "Oh, stop being so modest."

"You look fabulous, my dear. Are you married to anyone these days?"

"No, but I'm getting married."

"To whom?"

"Douglas Worthington."

"Who's he?"

Her eyes widened. "You mean you don't know who Douglas Worthington is? Where do you live, in a closet? Don't you read newspapers?"

"Who is he?"

"He's just been appointed Ambassador to the Court of Saint James."

Butler smiled. "Gee, you're really going first class these days, huh Brenda?"

"I've been going first class ever since I terminated my so-called marriage to you, Butler."

"I believe you have it wrong, my dear. I'm the one who terminated the marriage to you."

"Your memory has grown fuzzy," she said huffily.

"Then let me go over the facts with you, if you don't mind. The place was Argentina and the year was 1972. I was a case officer in the CIA station in Buenos Aires, and I caught you in bed with..."

"Don't be cruel," she interrupted. "Let's not dredge up depressing memories that no longer have any vital significance. What's done is done and what's over is over. I bear you no malice and you should bear me none. After all, we're civilized people, aren't we?"

"We most certainly are." Her perfume was making him dizzy, and he wanted to bury his face in her bosom, those two milky-white soft things that once belonged to him and him alone, or so he thought until he learned otherwise.

She was still studying his face. "You know," she said in a faraway voice, "you were by far the most interesting of my husbands. Now I didn't say the most intelligent, and I didn't say the best-looking, nor did I say the most charming or witty, but I did say the most interesting by far."

"In what way?"

She glanced around them, and they were in the middle of a stream of bellboys carrying the luggage of well-dressed people. Returning her gaze to Butler, she smiled alluringly and said, "Let's have a drink together, and I'll explain."

Butler felt trapped and scared. He was worried that if he spent more than a few minutes with her he'd fall in love with her all over again. She was still that stunning.

"I don't think we should," he replied in a halting voice.

"What's wrong?"

"Well, what's over is over, I suppose."

"You're not afraid of me, are you?"

"Who me?"

She laughed. "Why, I do believe that you are afraid of me." She laughed again. "You're so funny. You're also the

124

funniest of all my husbands. Did you know that?"

"No."

She took him by the sleeve. "Come have a drink with me. Please?" She gazed into his eyes, and he was utterly defeated.

"Okay," he said.

They walked across the plush old lobby and entered the dark Albemarle Bar, a gathering place for diplomats, scientists, and old money. Selecting a table in a corner, they sat and a portly old waiter came hurrying over.

"A martini, very dry," said Brenda.

"A double shot of Canadian Club, no ice, with a water back," Butler told the waiter.

The waiter floated off into the darkness with his order, and Brenda turned to Butler. "Still drinking your whisky straight, eh?"

"Yep."

"Still a tough sonofabitch, huh, Butler?"

"You betcha."

She touched her long fingers to his mighty shoulders. "You were okay, Butler."

"So were you, Brenda."

"Too bad it didn't work out, huh?"

"Yeah."

"We had fun together."

"Yes," Butler agreed, feeling melancholy. "We had fun together."

"If you hadn't been so old-fashioned and straight-laced, we would probably still be together today."

He shrugged. "I guess so, but I didn't believe in sharing my wife with half the diplomats and politicians in Buenos Aires."

"You had a very narrow-minded view of marriage. You were so selfish. You wanted me all to yourself, and you should realize, Butler dear, that I can't belong to any one man."

"I know that now."

"I need to be free as a bird," she said with a wave of her hand.

"Promiscuous as an alley cat might be the more appropriate metaphor."

"Did you really think I was promiscuous, Butler dear?"

"How could I possibly avoid that conclusion?"

"Am I a nymphomaniac?"

"I'm not a psychologist. All I know is that you fuck around too much. And people who trivialize sex tend to trivialize all human relationships."

"I don't trivialize sex at all. I think it's very important."

"When you do it all the time with all types of different people, you trivialize it. It becomes an ordinary human function, like taking a shit, instead of something exalted and fine."

"You're so old-fashioned." She smiled tenderly. "I think that's one of the things I liked about you. Beneath that rough exterior, there beats the heart of a gentleman."

"Oh, come on."

"It's true. It's getting warm in here. I think I'll take off my coat."

She stood and turned her back to him, waiting for him to help her take it off, and he did his duty, removing the black mouton fur from her remarkable shoulders. She sat again, her fur hat still on, and she looked like a kind of cossack queen. She wore a silky emerald-colored dress with a bodice low enough to show just a bit of her scrumptious breasts. Butler did some quick mental arithmetic and figured that she was thirty-one years old, a good age for women because they're usually less silly and more compassionate at that age.

The waiter came with the drinks, set them on the table with a series of little flourishes, and receded into the darkness of the cocktail lounge.

"Let's drink a toast, Butler," she said, picking up her martini in her elegant fingers.

He held his glass of whisky. "To what?"

"To love, what else?"

He laughed. "Okay. To love."

"Why are you laughing?"

"Because you don't know what love is."

126

"I don't know what love is?" she said, raising her eyebrows. "I think I know much more about love than you. I've had much more experience."

"You think because you fuck around a lot, you are the high priestess of love, but really all you are is a woman who fucks around a lot."

She held her glass bravely in the air. "To love?"

Butler touched her glass with his. "To love, that most precious and elusive thing."

"How eloquent you can be, Butler," she said.

"Only because you inspire me so, madame."

They each took a sip from their glasses, then placed them on the table and looked at each other. Butler thought how strange love could be, because he had lived with this woman and knew all her nasty habits, and had seen her many times sitting on toilet bowls, had seen her sick, feverish, and vomiting, had found her in bed with other men, had gone through a long, ugly divorce with her, and yet still, despite all that, he still could feel enchanted by her presence.

"What are you thinking?" she asked.

"I was thinking that in a certain part of my mind, I still love you despite everything."

"Do you really?"

"I really do."

"That's beautiful, Butler. Maybe you're the only man who ever really loved me."

"Oh, I doubt that."

"I mean it. It's very possible. Other men—I'm not sure they even knew who I was. But you—you knew who I was. Yes, you really knew who I was."

"To my regret."

"Oh, I wasn't that bad, Butler."

"You broke my heart, Brenda. I was a romantic young man when I met you, and now I'm just a cynic. Ever since we parted I've been a cynic. I don't think I ever could trust another woman."

She laughed gaily. "That's good. Because you never should trust women that much. Women and men are much different, and are always working at cross purposes. We want different things from each other, therefore no man should ever trust a woman, and no woman should ever trust a man. I have taught you something very valuable. You should thank me."

"Thanks a lot."

"Do you have a girl friend now, Butler? Tell me about her."

"I don't have a girlfriend. I just fuck around a lot, but unlike you, I don't get married."

"I've only been married four times."

"And this one will be your fifth."

"Yes, and you've been married once after you married me. She was a Mexican, somebody told me."

"Venezuelan."

"Rich or poor?"

"Very rich."

"Those are the best kind."

"On the contrary, I think those are the worst kind. She was spoiled, selfish, and crazy."

"But you loved her?"

"Yes."

"More than you loved me?"

"How could I possibly love anyone more than I loved you?"

She smiled. "You're sweet, Butler. You don't mean it, but it's nice of you to say it anyway. I really did care for you, Butler. Really I did. And you were by far the most interesting of all my husbands."

"That's right too—you were going to tell me why. That's why we came in here in the first place."

She cocked an eye. "Do you really want to know?"

"Yes, I really want to know."

"And what will you give me for the information? I know that you're a spy, and that you're accustomed to paying for information."

"I'm not a spy anymore," Butler said flatly.

"No?"

"No."

"You mean you've left the Agency?"

"Correct."

"What are you doing now?"

"General security work for a scientific organization."

"Must be pretty dull for you."

"It's nice to take it easy for a change."

"Sure it is." She winked and dug her elbow into his ribs.

"What's that supposed to mean?"

She winked again. "Deep cover, huh?"

"What do you mean?"

"Oh come on, you know you're still with the Agency. You don't have to lie to me. I'm not the enemy, for crying out loud. I'm your first wife, Brenda, remember? I was with you in Argentina, remember? I know all about your tricky little life."

"Okay, I'm still with the Agency."

"Good. I'd be disappointed if I knew you had an ordinary life. I have this fantasy about you, you see. You are doing secret work, risking your life in strange foreign countries, and nobody knows who you are. I know it's not true, but I like to think it anyway. And do you want to know what else I like to think? I like to think that no matter what you do and no matter where you go, deep in your heart you still are in love with me."

Butler nodded and sipped his drink. "What a delusion all that is."

"I know, but I like to think it. It gives me comfort and peace."

"You still haven't told me why I'm more interesting than your other twenty husbands."

"Four, darling. Going on five. What makes you so interesting?" She looked at his face, as though searching for the answer there. "Because you're brave, sensitive, and idealistic, and yet you appear to be nothing more than some sort of high class gangster."

"That's all a spy is, really. A high class gangster."

"But it's not all you are. You would die for something you believed in—yes, you would, don't deny it."

"Okay, I won't deny it."

"Most men wouldn't, you know, because most men don't believe in anything, not even themselves. You believe in yourself, Butler. You know your strengths and weaknesses. You know when to push and when to back off. You're not a fool, although sometimes you like to act like one. Your life rests on a moral foundation, and that makes you very attractive to people like me who have no morals at all."

Butler laughed. "You admit it!"

"Of course I admit it! Why shouldn't I admit the truth?"

"If you feel that you must admit the truth, then you must have morals someplace."

"I have no morals, only a sense of expediency. I do what seems right for me at the moment, because I believe that we only live once and don't get a second chance to run around the track. Life is too short to deny oneself the little pleasures that are so rare and beautiful. I don't believe in sin. Sin is bullshit."

"I don't believe in sin either, but I do believe in the consequences of actions. People who do bad things pay for it in the end. One way or another, they pay. And you, my dear, will pay one day too. And so will I, because in some matters I'm not as moral as you suppose."

"You are referring no doubt to sexual matters."

"Yes."

"But you're a free man. You can screw whomever you like. So why shouldn't you have your fun?"

"Because as I told you before, when you trivialize sex, you trivialize everything."

"Nonsense."

"Is it? Think about it."

"I don't want to think about it. It's depressing."

"You can't hide from your mind."

"Oh, stop it," she said crossly.

"You want me to leave?"

"No, don't leave." She shrugged away the encroaching bad mood. "Tell me something pretty."

"You're pretty."

"I am? Still?"

"Yes, and you know it."

"I don't know it." She frowned. "I'm growing old."

"You're such a little idiot."

"I am growing old."

"You're not getting older. You're getting better."

She brightened. "Am I really?"

"Yes. I still could fall in love with you if I let myself."

"Let yourself."

"Never."

"Why not?"

"Because I'm only one ordinary human being, not a tank."

She looked at him in the candlelight flickering on the table. "You know, you're not bad-looking at all."

"You know, people tell me that from time to time. I think it means that I'm ugly, but not that ugly."

"No, you're really quite handsome, but in a masculine way, not a pretty pretty boy way. Your hair is so thick and black and healthy. I'd love to run my fingers through it."

"Go ahead."

"You'd like it, wouldn't you."

"You're damn right I would."

"You're still in love with me, aren't you?"

"Of course I am."

She smiled mischievously. "Why don't you do something about it?"

"Like what?"

"You tell me."

He looked into her eyes. "Don't tempt me."

She showed him her tongue. "I'm tempting you."

"If you don't stop that, I'll take you upstairs and screw your brains out."

"Oh, Butler, dare we?"

"Dare? There wouldn't be anything daring about it at all."

She closed her eyes. "When I think of myself in bed with you, I get mushy all over. You were such a good lover, Butler. I loved it when you went down on me. You used to make me so crazy that I didn't even know who I was."

"You loved me so much that whenever I was out of sight you jumped into bed with the nearest available sonofabitch."

"I really was just a child when I married you, Butler. I didn't know anything about life and love, and you ignited such a wild passion in me that when you were gone for long periods of time, I had to quench it somehow. But it was all your fault. If you hadn't been such a good lover, I still might be your little housewife to this day."

"You never were my little housewife. You always were farting around someplace."

"Well, you were supposed to be a member of the diplomatic corps. Therefore it was my duty, as your wife, to be sociable."

"You were supposed to be sociable, but not sexual."

She smiled and fluttered her eyelashes. "I admit I do get those two categories mixed up a little bit at times."

He looked at her, and she was such a silly, beautiful creature, with her golden hair and her dashing hat. He knew every square inch of her body; it should have no mystery for him anymore, and yet it did. The thought of it filled his mind with eroticism.

"Let's go upstairs," he said.

A look of triumph came over her face. "Is that a proposition?"

"It certainly isn't a proposal."

"Do you really think we should?"

"A few moments ago you were wiggling your tongue at me, and now you're asking if we should? Why are you so fucking crazy, Brenda?"

She bared her teeth at him. "Because I want to drive you mad with lust."

"I am already mad with lust."

"You don't look it."

"What am I supposed to do, foam at the mouth?"

"Yes."

"I can't foam at the mouth."

"Then do something else. Make a scene. Kiss my feet. Punch somebody."

Butler raised his hand, and the waiter materialized out of the darkness like a ghost from the spirit world.

"You called, sir?"

"My check, please."

"Yes, sir."

The waiter tallied up the check and gave it to Butler, who glanced at it, took a role of bills from his pocket, and threw the waiter a twenty. "Keep the change."

"Thank you, sir."

The waiter disappeared again, and Butler stood up, buttoning his suit jacket. "Let's go."

"Say please."

"Please."

"Say pretty please."

He bent over and grabbed her tightly by the wrist. "I said let's go."

"You're hurting me," she whined.

"I'll break your neck if you don't get a move on."

She looked around. "You're making a scene."

"You like that, don't you?"

"Yes."

"You're a little pervert, aren't you, beneath that beautiful, icy exterior."

"Yes, but all I am today, I owe to you."

"Horseshit."

She stood and smoothed the front of her dress. He draped her mouton coat over her shoulders, and hooked her arm in his. Then he led her out of the lounge and across the lobby to the elevator, where he pressed the button.

"Let me go," she said in a low voice.

"No."

"What if my fiance shows up?"

"I'll punch him right in the mouth."

"Now I'm starting to get a little scared."

"You opened this can of beans, not me."

The elevator came and they got on with a number of people, all well-dressed and elegant. Butler was reminded of the St. Regis Hotel in New York as the elevator rose. It made various stops and finally came to the fourteenth floor, where Butler's room was.

They got off the elevator and walked down the corridor to the room.

"I feel so wicked," Brenda said with a shiver.

"Then you must be happy."

"I am. And filled with anticipation of the sexual splendors that you shall visit upon me forthwith." She rolled her eyes and licked her lips, then giggled at her silliness.

He opened the appropriate door and they entered the dark suite of rooms. He flicked on a light and saw a comfortable little drawing room with sofas, chairs, and a fireplace. Adjacent to the drawing room was the bedroom, where Butler pulled Brenda by her wrist.

"Let me go," she pleaded, not very convincingly.

He spun her around, wrapped his arms around her slender waist, and pulled her toward him. She melted, moaned and raised her lips to his. They kissed, opened their mouths, touched tongues, and got dizzy. Butler reached behind her dress for her zipper, and pulled it down. He stepped away from her and saw the top of her dress fall away from her delicious, floppy breasts. He took one of them in his hand, bent over, and kissed its little point. Brenda closed her eyes and moaned. Butler picked her up and placed her in the middle of the bed, then pulled down her dress, slip, and underpants.

She lay naked on the bed except for her cossack hat, which she reached towards with her hands. "I'll take this off," she said.

"No, leave it on."

"You like it on?"

"Yes."

"We're getting very kinky, aren't we dear?"

"Getting?"

134

Butler took off his suit jacket and threw it across the room. Then he peeled away his shirt, and she looked at his powerful chest covered with pectoral muscles nearly as big as pineapples.

"Still going to the gym, I see."

"Whenever I can," he replied, dropping his pants.

The Colt .45 hit the floor with a thud.

"Was that your gun?" she asked.

"It wasn't my cock."

"Would you put it under the pillow, just like in the old days?"

"What, my cock?"

"No, the gun."

He chuckled as he bent over naked and picked it up. "Sure." He got onto the bed and tucked the Colt under the pillow. "Happy now?"

"I can't help it if guns turn me on. I suppose you think that's sick."

"If you're sick, then what am I?"

"Sicker."

"Right." He lay on top of her and gazed into her smoldering eyes. "Have you ever thought of me when you made love to other men?"

"Many times."

"What did you think?"

"I thought of what a good lay you were, Butler. You really were a very good lay. Too bad you had to spend so much time away from home."

"Too bad you're such a little sex degenerate." He brought his hand between her legs, and she shuddered. "Look how wet you are already."

"Do it to me, Butler, before I die," she said huskily.

He laughed sardonically. "What would you do if I walked out of here right now?"

"I'd kill you, but you wouldn't do that to me, would you, Butler?"

"I couldn't do it to myself," he replied.

He kissed her eyes, her lips, and her ears. He ran his

135

tongue over her lips, then went between them to her tongue that tasted like wine. She undulated like an ocean underneath him, and he kissed her beauteous breasts, licked her belly button, and then went down to the center of her femininity, that fragile, delicate place surrounded with gold curls.

She grabbed fistfuls of his hair, and thrashed about on the bed. He held her lissome legs tightly and slurped her up, and soon she was screaming and yelping, her eyes rolling up into her head.

"Oh, Butler," she sighed. "What you do to me is a crime."

He licked his way up her writhing body to her lips, and she spread her legs because she was hungry for the feel of him inside her. He slid right in, just like the old days, and her vagina held him tight as a fist.

"I've always loved you," she whispered, swaying her hips from side to side. "I've never forgotten you. You've always been the only man for me."

"Sssshhh," he said, moving in and out of her, not wanting her to say things that she'd repudiate later, as she'd done so many times before.

18

It was one o'clock in the morning. They'd stopped making love a half hour ago, and now Butler was dozing off, thinking of all the ways he'd made love to her, and all ways she'd made love to him. It had been wonderful, just like the old days, but in the morning she was supposed to go horseback riding with her new fiance, and he was supposed to go to the Institute for the meeting to decide what to do about the Doom Machine. Their paths had converged for a brief moment, but soon they'd be off on separate directions, perhaps never to meet again.

A scraping sound came from the terrace. Butler raised his head so he could hear better. Then it sounded as though something was dropped out there. He reached under the pillow for the Colt .45, then pushed the covers away and got out of bed.

"Where are you going?" she asked sleepily.

"Sssshhhh. There's someone on the terrace."

"What!"

"Sssshhhh. Be still. I'll see what's going on."

Naked as a jaybird, Butler tiptoed across the rug to the terrace door. Pressing his back to the wall beside the door, he peeked through the curtains and saw shadowy figures out there. He'd have to act fast; this was no time to fool around. Bounding in front of the terrace door, he pulled it open abruptly and pointed his gun.

"Don't move!" he said.

Three men in topcoats and slouch hats were on the terrace, gathering together electrical gear and cameras. Beside them was a rope ladder that led to the terrace of the apartment above. The three men were taken by surprise, and the one whose jaw hung open the widest was none other than F.J. Shankham, Director of Current Intelligence for the CIA.

"Hello Butler," Shankham said with an uncertain smile.

"What the fuck are you doing out here, Shankham!"

"Oh, just getting a bit of fresh air," Shankham said nonchalantly. "By the way, let me introduce my two friends, Dudley Farnsworth and Timothy Pickering, of my office.

"Hi there," said Dudley, around twenty-six years old.

"Pleased to meet you," said Timothy, extending his hand.

Butler ignored the both of them and looked at Shankham. Stars sparkled in the sky and the sound of traffic could be heard below. A breeze covered Butler's nude body with goose bumps, and made his pecker shrivel up.

"What are you doing spying on me, Shankham!" Butler demanded.

Shankham smiled and held out the palms of his hands. His coat collar was up and his slouch hat was low over his eyes. "Well, you know how it is, Butler. People get assignments and people go out on them."

"What do you want with me, you cruddy bastard!"

"Oh, this and that."

"This and what?"

"We just were wondering what you were up to, since you just got back from the Soviet Union and all."

"I was getting laid, and that was none of your business."

"But you know how it is, Butler. You never know what a person's liable to say in a moment of passion. We've got a lot of very valuable intelligence that way, but of course, I don't have to tell you that. You were one of our greatest master spies, for crying out loud. You wrote the book, for goodness sakes."

Butler was shivering wildly and thought he might catch pneumonia if he stayed on the terrace. "Get inside, you three. And bring your junk with you."

"What are you going to do with us, Butler. Surely you're not going to do anything silly."

"I said, get inside!"

The men picked up their equipment and carried it into the hotel room. Brenda turned on the light beside the bed and pulled the covers up over her boobs. Her hair was mussed and all her makeup was gone, but she still looked delectable.

"Who are all these people!" she demanded.

"Permit me to introduce myself," said F.J. Shankham, tipping his hat. "My name is Shankham and I'm an old friend of your husband's."

"Old friend, my ass," Butler growled. "You're no friend of mine, Shankham."

"Colleague, then."

Butler looked at Brenda. "They're all in the CIA, and they've been taking pictures and making recordings of us."

Her eyes goggled. "What!"

"That's what they've been doing," Butler said with resignation.

"Oh, my goodness!" Brenda said, holding her palms to her cheeks. "I'm so embarrassed!"

Dudley Farnsworth and Timothy Pickering looked at each other and grinned. Shankham shrugged.

"What can I tell you?" he asked.

Butler pointed his gun at him. "I ought to shoot the three of you for criminal trespass."

Shankham blanched. "Now Butler..."

"I really should," Butler continued. "I'd probably get away with it, too. You are, after all, trespassing criminally."

"Yes, they are," Brenda agreed.

Butler aimed the Colt at Shankham.

"NO!" screamed Shankham, holding out his hands.

Butler lowered his gun. "I'm not going to shoot you, you worm. I couldn't shoot a man in cold blood."

"I'm so happy to hear that, Butler."

"You're just going to turn all your film and all your tapes over to me."

"Now Butler..."

"Come on!"

"But you know that I have to account for all this material. What will I tell them when they ask what happened?"

"Tell them the truth—that I caught you, you bastard."

"But that'll ruin my career!"

"You'll bounce back. All you CIA hacks eventually do. Come on, hand it over before I start shooting, dammit!"

Shankham looked at Farnsworth and Pickering. "Give them what they want."

Farnsworth opened the movie camera and took out the reel of film, while Pickering opened a satchel and took out more film plus some tape cartridges. They placed the stuff on the floor before Butler, then stepped back sheepishly. Butler told them to put their hands in the air and turn around, and then he searched each of them, removing pistols, knives, laser pens, and various other implements of the spy trade.

"Okay," Butler said. "Now get the fuck out of here."

"Listen, Butler," Shankham said. "I really apologize for all this, but you know how it is."

"I know how it is. Just get out of here before I lose my temper."

Shankham tipped his hat to Brenda. "Good night, madame. Awfully sorry about all this. By the way, don't I know you from somewhere?"

"No," replied Brenda coldly.

"I could swear that I've seen you in the company of Douglas Worthington, the new Ambassador to the Court of Saint James."

"Never heard of him."

"Well good night."

"Good night to you. And it's very bad manners to spy on people while they're being intimate with each other."

"What I do, I do for my country, madame."

Butler pointed at the door with his gun. "Get out of here, you lying sack of shit."

Shankham scurried to the door, with Farnsworth and Pickering close behind him, carrying their cameras and tape recorders. They left the hotel room, and Butler locked the door behind them.

"What a bunch of scumbags," he said.

Brenda let the covers fall from her alabaster breasts. "I've met that Shankham before at a reception someplace. What if he tells Douglas about us?"

"He won't because that'll blow his cover. If you ever meet him again you'll both pretend that you never met." Butler kneeled beside the piles of film and tapes. "I'll have to take this with me tomorrow and destroy it."

"Oh, let's keep it, Butler. We can have it developed and see what we look like."

"That's not a good idea, because it's liable to fall into the wrong hands someday."

She frowned. "I suppose you're right. Well, come to bed."

"Yes, I have to get up early tomorrow."

"Me too. I must go riding with Douglas at daybreak, and I'll be so sore because I've been riding with you all night."

Butler turned off the light and crawled into bed with her.

"Can I kiss it good night?" she asked.

"Go ahead."

She pushed the covers away and kneeled over it. "It's sleeping," she said.

"It's tired."

"I'll bet I could wake him up."

"I'll bet you could too."

She lowered her head and gave it a big wet kiss, and sure enough it began to wake up.

"Here we go again," Butler sighed.

"Well, it's not as though we do it every day," she replied, but Butler couldn't understand her very well, because her mouth was full.

141

19

At nine o'clock in the morning, Butler reported to Mr. Sheffield's office, carrying a shopping bag full of film and recording tape.

"Good morning, Butler," Mister Sheffield said in the dark room. "I trust you slept well?"

"Not that well. I had a visitation from the CIA."

"Sit down and tell me about it."

Butler sat down, placing the shopping bag beside him. "There's not much to tell, really. I happened to be in bed with a certain young lady, and I became aware of noise out on the terrace. I investigated and found three CIA agents with cameras and tape recorders. I confiscated the film and tape, and I'll want someone here to destroy them, because they would be very damaging to the young lady's reputation."

"I quite understand. When you're finished here, you may take them down to the furnace."

"Good."

"Did the CIA people say why they were there?"

"Not really, but it had something to do with my experiences in the Soviet Union."

"I see. Well then, if they're watching you, you'll have to go underground, won't you?"

"Why will I have to go underground?"

"Because this evening you're leaving on a mission of the

utmost importance, and we wouldn't want the CIA to know about that, would we?"

"No, we wouldn't. Where am I going?"

"To Damascus, with another agent, an Egyptian named Farouk Moussa. He speaks Arabic fluently, it is his native language, and you will be in charge of the mission. You will have two objectives. The first will be to sabotage the part of the Abdul Faheem Munitions Works that is manufacturing the Doom Machines. The second is to obtain the plans for the Doom Machine somehow. This second objective will be your most difficult, but you must carry it out. We have no idea where the plans might be. You must find them somehow and bring them back so that we can disseminate them among the countries of the world that don't have access to the Doom Machine themselves."

"The Doom Machine project is probably being directed by a team of Russian scientists. If we can get to one of them, perhaps we can get to the plans."

"Good thinking, Butler."

"The best way to get to someone is to do it through a beautiful woman. Even the most rational man will do silly things in the company of a beautiful woman."

"I take it you're speaking from experience, Butler."

"Very bitter experience, sir. Do we have a skilled female agent who can come with us?"

"Hmmm, let me think." Sheffield shuffled some papers on his desk, and Butler noticed his thin white hands unadorned by rings or even a wrist watch. "I believe that Wilma B. Willoughby is here in Washington."

"Wilma B. Willoughby!" Butler explained.

"Yes, surely you remember her."

"Of course I remember her. The Institute sent her to check me out when you were thinking of recruiting me."

"Yes, she's a most competent agent, and she speaks numerous foreign languages, even Arabic, fluently. Moreover, she can speak, for example, Russian with a French accent, French with a German accent, and Russian with an Arabic accent. She's a very clever agent. Would you like to take her with you?"

"Um, I don't know."

"Why don't you know?"

"Well, we're sort of friendly."

"You mean you've had sexual relations with *her* too?"

"No."

"Ah, I see," Mister Sheffield said sagely. "The problem is that you *haven't* had sexual relations with her. You attempted to seduce her, but it didn't work. Am I right?"

"You're right."

"And therefore you feel somewhat insecure in her presence?"

"Right again."

"I see. Well really, Butler, I think you have to put your personal feelings aside at a time like this. Why, the fate of the world hangs in the balance here. Wilma is the only female agent we have available at this particular moment. You've got to take her with you."

"Well, if I've got to take her with me, I guess I've got to take her with me," Butler said.

"Good thinking, Butler old man. Well, we don't have a moment to lose. Mr. Jahrum of our Middle East department will brief you on the details of your mission, and tonight I suspect you'll be leaving for Syria. Good luck, Butler. Give it the best you've got, because..."

"I know," Butler interrupted. "The fate of the world hangs in the balance here."

"Exactly," said Sheffield.

20

The long black submarine motored underneath the waters of the Mediterranean Sea. Captain Sinclair looked through the periscope and saw shells bursting in the beleaguered city of Beirut. The Lebanese Civil War had erupted again, but it was decided to drop Butler and his cohorts in Lebanon and let them make their way east to Damascus, because that would be shorter than dropping them in northern Syria, which was much farther from Damascus than Beirut.

"The shelling is still quite heavy," said Captain Sinclair.

"Good," said Butler. "Everybody will be too busy fighting to notice us."

"I hope you're right," said Farouk Moussa, the Egyptian with a long face and black curly hair. He was a few inches taller than Butler and was twenty-eight years old. Before joining the Institute he'd been a teacher of physical education at the University of North Carolina.

"He's probably wrong," said Wilma B. Willoughy, a cute little bitch if ever there was one. She had straight black hair and the face of an angel, which she most assuredly was not.

During their day of briefing and flight to Tel Aviv, where they boarded the submarine, Butler and Wilma had been studiously polite to each other, although Wilma had rejected his offer of sexual love some months ago, and he had stood

145

her up on a date shortly thereafter. However, since boarding the submarine, hostility had been growing between them.

"Why do you think I'm wrong?" Butler asked her.

"My female intuition."

"You know what you can do with your female intuition."

"We'll see who's right and who's wrong."

"We sure will."

"I wish you two would cut it out," Farouk said.

Butler pointed his finger at her. "Stop talking back to me. This is a very important mission, and I'm the boss. You heard Mr. Sheffield say that I'm the boss. So stop hassling me."

She thumbed her nose at him.

Captain Sinclair cleared his throat . "We're about two hundred yards from the docks of Beirut. Are you ready to go ashore?"

"We're ready when you are, Captain," Butler said.

Captain Sinclair looked at Lieutenant Jordan. "Take her up."

"Take her up," repeated Lieutenant Jordan.

Sailors at the consoles twirled dials and pulled levers. Butler felt the front of the submarine point upwards. The crew was ready and waiting with the rubber boat and oars. Butler, Farouk, and Wilma wore black camouflage outfits over traditional Arab garb, and underneath the Arab garb they carried plastic demolition materials, blasting caps, guns, knives, radios, laser pens, and various other implements common to the trade of secret agents.

The submarine leveled off and the crew members ran up the ladderwells like monkeys. Butler, Farouk, and Wilma followed them up, with Captain Sinclair close behind. The sailor on top opened the hatch and they all spilled out onto the deck. Butler heard shells exploding while he still was in the submarine, and when he came up to the conning tower, he could see that the city of Beirut was burning and shattering before his eyes. The Christians and Moslems still were trying to kill each other, and neither side would make the slightest concession. It was another example of the human race gone insane.

The sailors tossed the rubber boat over the side, then handed ropes to Butler, Farouk, and Wilma.

"Good luck," Captain Sinclair said, shaking their hands.

Farouk went over the side first and got in the rubber boat. Wilma went next, and then came Butler. They cast off the lines and sailors aboard the submarine gathered them up. Farouk took the oars in hand and started rowing toward shore, while Wilma sat in the front of the rubber boat and Butler sat in back, watching buildings explode and topple to the ground in Beirut.

"Am I headed in the right direction?" Farouk asked, squinting ahead.

"Yes," replied Butler. "The fishing boats are straight ahead."

"You're sure?"

"Yes, I'm sure."

Wilma pointed her long, elegant finger toward shore. "I think the fishing boats are farther to the left."

"They are not," Butler said. "Please pipe down."

She gave him a dirty look that Butler could perceive even on the dark and moonless night. Farouk continued pushing toward shore, and in back of them the submarine slipped beneath the waves. They were alone now and moving ever closer to wartorn Beirut.

When they were about halfway to shore, Butler said, "I'll take the oars now."

"I'm not tired yet," Farouk replied.

"I said I'll take the oars."

"He said he's not tired," Wilma chimed in.

"Listen here, you two," Butler said through clenched teeth, for he was getting angry. "I'm in command here, and I don't want any more back talk. Is that clear?"

"Yes," said Farouk.

"Uh-huh," said Wilma.

"Then change places with me, Farouk."

"But I'm not tired yet."

In motions so fast his hands were a blur, Butler reached under his clothes and pulled out his Colt .45. "I'm going to blow your fucking brains out if you don't do as you're told," he said to Farouk, pointing the gun at his nose. "You're endangering my life and the success of this mission with your bullshit."

"I just realized that I'm tired," Farouk said, staring into the mouth of the gun.

He got up and exchanged places with Butler, who kneeled between the oars, picked them up, and started rowing. Wilma was sitting on her knees in front of him, and he looked over her shoulder and saw the masts of the fishing boats straight ahead. He pushed toward them, and as the rubber boat drew closer, he saw that the old scows were tied up side by side to each other, making floating piers that extended into the water.

Buildings close to the waterfront were ablaze, and Butler was worried that they'd be seen. Machine guns chattered within the depths of the city, and rifle fire could be heard from all directions. He rowed toward a line of fishing boats.

"Keep your heads down," he said. "Farouk, get your knife out. I'm going to row toward those fishing boats, and we'll climb aboard one. I want you to puncture holes in this rubber boat so that it'll sink, and then as soon as we get on the fishing boat, we have to get rid of all this camouflage gear, got it?"

"Got it," Farouk said.

"How about you, Ms. Willoughby?"

"Got it."

Butler rowed toward the fishing boats. Slowly he closed the distance between the rubber boat and them. Finally they approached the last boat at the end of the pier.

"Grab the boat," Butler told Wilma as they glided closer.

Wilma grabbed the gunwale of the fishing boat.

"Sink this fucking thing!" Butler told Farouk.

Farouk had his knife out and plunged it into the rubber boat. Butler took his old British commando bayonet out and did the same thing. The rubber boat hissed and began to sink into the Mediterranean Sea.

"Abandon ship!" Butler said.

Butler, Farouk, and Wilma jumped from the rubber boat onto the fishing boat. Turning around, they saw the rubber boat sputter and bubble and sink beneath the waves. Then they removed their black camouflage clothing and threw them after the rubber boat. Now, in flowing Arabian robes and burnooses, with Wilma wearing a veil over her face, they scrambled over the fishing boats toward the central dock, but upon nearing it, a figure with a rifle loomed up at them out of the darkness.

"Halt—who goes there!" the figure shouted.

"Poor fishing folk," Farouk replied, bowing.

Butler and Wilma also bowed, to show their respect and humility.

"Where's your fish?" asked the sentry.

"Alas, we have none. We have fished all night, and caught nothing. Perhaps the war is scaring the fish away."

"Come up here, and let me look at you."

They climbed from the fishing boat onto the dock, and the sentry looked them over. The sentry wore a khaki uniform and cloth cap, and it couldn't be discerned whether he was a Christian, a Moslem, or what.

"Get on with your business," the sentry said at last. "And hereafter, don't be slinking around the docks. You're liable to be shot by mistake."

"Yes, sir. Thank you, sir."

Butler, Farouk, and Wilma bowed and moved off toward the burning city of Beirut. They walked quickly, the men on the outside and Wilma between them.

"That was too close for comfort," Butler said. "We're lucky the man was cool-headed. Otherwise he'd have shot first and asked questions afterwards."

Wilma looked ahead at the flames and shellbursts. "How are we going to get through all that?"

"I don't know. We'll have to get a vehicle from someplace."

The three undercover agents entered the devastated city of Beirut. They passed through the financial district, which was utterly demolished, and a bit farther, saw Moslems and Christians fighting for control of the Holiday Inn. Skirting the perimeter of the battle, they continued west. At one point they had to hide in an alley filled with rubble, while motorized detachments of one of the armies went past. They left the alley, and halfway down the block, they saw a dead child lying in the gutter. The child was no more than twelve, its chest caked with blood, its eyes wide open and staring. This is the face of war, Butler thought.

They continued through the shelling and machine gun fire, dashing from shelter to shelter. Once they had to take cover in a cellar filled with the refugees of the war. Another time they hid in a sewer with a family that had been living there since the war began. And once, in a cemetery, they huddled behind gravestones as shells burst all around them. Butler looked around the gravestone at Beirut covered with sheets of flame, and thought that the whole world might look like that if this mission failed.

On the other side of the cemetery, they saw a jeep that had hit a telephone pole. The driver and two passengers were lying in the middle of the road with bullet holes through them; evidently they'd been ambushed. The engine of the jeep was still running.

"It looks like this might be our vehicle," Butler said, jumping into the cockpit.

The gearshift lever was in neutral; the driver must have been braking when he'd been shot. Butler shifted into reverse, and to his gratification, the jeep backed away from the telephone pole. He pulled up the emergency brake, got out, and checked the front damage. There wasn't much, only a dented fender and grille. The radiator and engine were still intact.

"Pile in," Butler said. "I'll drive."

Farouk got beside Butler on the front seat, and Wilma sat in back. Butler gunned the engine, shifted into gear, and sped off in the direction of the Syrian border. But to get there, they still had to pass through a considerable portion of Beirut. Butler steered around heaps of corpses and the rubble of buildings. He drove down streets lined with burning buildings. On Kalif Avenue there was a roadblock, but Butler veered around it and kept on going. They ducked their heads as bullets whizzed all around them, but Butler kept going and soon the little jeep was out of range.

As the sun rose in the east behind them, they were clearing the outskirts of Beirut and heading for the desert. The Syrian border was only fifty miles away, and Damascus only about twenty-five miles beyond that. They entered the desert, and soon the tumult of Beirut could no longer be heard. They passed Arabs riding camels, and little oases in the middle of nowhere. The air was hot and still, and sweat poured off their bodies.

"It seems to me," Wilma said, "that it would have been much easier if we'd just flown directly to Damascus."

"With the explosives?" Butler asked.

"That's right too. I forgot about the explosives."

"If the Syrian customs people found the explosives on us, we would go directly to jail, and the last place any of us want to be is in a Syrian jail. Lawrence of Arabia was in a Syrian jail, and we all know what happened to him."

"What was that?" Wilma asked.

"He was sodomized."

"Ugh."

They stopped at the next oasis for water and to eat some of the protein bars they'd brought along with them. Butler consulted his maps and was able to determine that they were only ten miles from the Syrian border. Wilma took off her burnoose and shook out her lustrous black hair. Farouk smoked an Egyptian cigarette and scratched his mustache. They sat in a circle around Butler's maps.

"We can't afford to take the chance of going through Customs," Butler said, "so we'll have to go off the road and drive over the desert, crossing the border at some remote point where they don't have guards."

"What if we get lost in the desert?" Wilma asked.

151

"We'll become food for the vultures, and then the sun will bleach our bones. Someday Bedouins will come upon us and wonder who we were."

"They will also wonder," Farouk said, "what we were doing with all the plastic bombs."

"They won't even know what they are," Butler replied. "I only hope they don't try to eat them, because they'll get very sick, and might even explode if they get too close to a fire."

"Very funny," Wilma said sarcastically.

Butler stood and folded his maps. "Fill the canteens with water, just in case." He checked his compass to make sure it was working all right. His plan was to drive in a southerly direction for a few miles, then head due east for about twenty miles, and finally swing north again, where he'd get on the same road they had been on, only it would be in Syria.

They got in the jeep and Butler steered off the road into the desert. The rear wheels kicked back spumes of sand as he sped along. It reminded Butler of a dune buggy he once drove in Southern California, but that had been close to Laguna Beach, and now he was in the Middle East, where death could come suddenly, viciously, and for no good reason.

The jeep zoomed across the desert. It climbed hills and zipped along the horizon, its three occupants hanging on for dear life. At noon with the sun a blazing ball directly overhead, Butler glanced at the speedometer and saw that they'd already come fifteen miles through the desert. Soon they'd swing north and get on the road to Damascus. He checked the fuel; there was plenty. The temperature gauge showed a normal reading, and Butler was reflecting happily on how well everything was going, when suddenly the radiator exploded, sending a geyser of hot water into the air. Butler was startled, and reflexively pulled the wheel to the right. The jeep spun around on the sand and came to a halt.

"Uh-oh," Butler said.

"I knew you were going too fast," Wilma told him accusingly.

"Much too fast," Farouk agreed.

"I was not going too fast. The problem was that the temperature needle evidently was broken."

Wilma sniffed the hot desert air. "The radiator would not have overheated if you weren't going so fast."

"We're not out here on a picnic," Butler reminded her. "We're on a mission of the utmost importance, and we can't afford to be leisurely."

"Haste makes waste," Wilma replied.

"If you keep bugging me, I'm going to waste you."

"You just try it, Buster."

"Oh shit," Butler replied, his shoulders sagging. This was why he always preferred to go on missions alone. You didn't have to put up with the bullshit of other people. "Okay," he said, trying to summon up the qualities of leadership. "There's no point in crying over spilt milk or broken radiators. Let's pull ourselves together and get moving."

Wilma hopped out of the jeep. "Some people just can't admit it when they're in the wrong," she said.

"It takes a real man to admit that he's wrong," Farouk added, adjusting his burnoose.

Butler was seriously tempted to take out his Colt .45 and blow them both away, but that would never do, and besides, he might need them at some point later on in the mission, although he couldn't imagine why he might need them later on. They both were a pain in the ass.

"Are we ready to move out?" Butler asked, wiping sweat from his forehead with his sleeve.

They nodded.

"Then let's go."

He headed in a northerly direction, where the road to Damascus was supposed to be.

"Are you sure this is the right direction?" Wilma asked.

"Quite sure."

"I think we should be going that way." She pointed toward the east.

"If you want to go that way, go that way."

"What makes you so sure I'm wrong?"

"My compass."

"Maybe your compass needle is off, just like the temperature needle in the jeep was off."

"Maybe your brain is off," Butler replied.

At this point Farouk decided to throw in his two cents. "You don't have to be insulting," he said insultingly.

"Shut your fucking mouth."

"What was that?"

"I said shut your fucking mouth, both of you."

"I think your remarks are most uncalled-for," said Farouk, who had lived in London for a time and spoke with a very proper British accent. "There is never any excuse for profanity."

"None whatsoever," Wilma agreed.

Butler wiped his nose with his sleeve. "I'm leaving in the direction I think we should go. You people can go wherever the fuck you want." He checked his compass again, then began trudging north. He kept his ears perked up, and heard them falling in behind him. They would argue and complain, but finally they would do what they were told. Things could be worse. They could always be worse. Especially in the desert.

Slowly and agonizingly they made their way toward the road to Damascus. The sun baked them and made their clothes stick to their bodies. Whenever they took a step, their feet sank into the sand and they had to pull them out. Their mouths became dry and they had to make numerous stops to drink water. Their legs ached and their lungs felt as though they were breathing the air inside a furnace. Butler found himself having fantasies of mint juleps and pitchers of lemonade. He saw himself in a bathing suit sitting beside the swimming pools of luxury hotels. He longed to stand in front of a highpowered air-conditioning unit.

"The asshole had to mess up the car," Wilma grumbled during one of their water breaks.

"I didn't mess up the car."

"If you didn't, who did?"

"The person who forgot to fix the temperature gauge."

154

"Go ahead, blame it on somebody else."

"Why don't you shut your big mouth?"

"Why don't you?"

Farouk shook his head. "You two are like a couple of children. You must be in love, the way you're arguing."

"In love!" Wilma spat out. "With him? Don't be absurd!"

Butler snorted. "The little bitch is half-crazy. Who could possibly love her?"

"Half-crazy, am I!" she screamed, crouching over and snarling at him. "Who are you calling half-crazy, you moron?"

Butler realized that the discipline of his little group was deteriorating rapidly. He had to take control and exercise command presence. "All right, let's move out!" he ordered in his best military officer voice.

"Listen to him," Wilma sneered. "He thinks he's back in the Army."

Butler decided to ignore her and start moving toward the Damascus Road. He knew they'd follow him, and sure enough, they did. Together they staggered across the desert, and Butler wondered where in the hell the road to Damascus was. He felt certain they should have reached it by now. The red ball of sun sank into the horizon on the west, and they were huffing and puffing like donkeys. It grew dark, and still they kept on, following the luminous needle on Butler's compass. Finally at around nine o'clock in the evening, Butler decided they'd better stop for the night. They were all tired and he was afraid they might walk right over the road in the dark and keep going.

"We'd better stop here for the night," he said, holding up his hand.

"Look at him," Wilma said wearily. "He looks like Chief Sitting Bull standing up there."

Butler shivered, for it gets cold on the desert at night. He wrapped his robes around him and sat on the sand. Taking out a protein bar, he unpeeled the wrapper and commenced to eat. Farouk and Wilma did the same, sitting near Butler.

"I think we're lost," Wilma said, munching her protein bar. "We should have gone that way." She pointed to the east, where a full moon was rising.

"If you want to go that way, go ahead," Butler told her.

"It's too late now," she said.

"It's never too late for anything," Butler replied.

Farouk took out a cigarette and lit up, smoking while eating his protein bar. "I don't know which way we should go, but we surely should have reached the Damascus Road by now."

Butler decided to say nothing. He was getting sick of arguing with his two companions. Bumming an Egyptian cigarette from Farouk, he leaned back against the sand dune and smoked it.

"I'm getting cold," Wilma said, rubbing her shoulders.

"No fires," Butler replied.

"It's strange how hot the desert is during the day, and how cold it gets at night."

"That is the way of the desert." Farouk said.

"But what is the way to the Damascus Road?" Wilma asked.

Butler pointed in the direction they were going. "That way."

"Wanna bet?" Wilma asked.

"No, because women never pay their debts. I recently won one hundred rubles from a woman and never got a penny of it."

Wilma stiffened her smile. "That remark is a slur against women everywhere."

Butler groaned and lay back. "Shut up—I'm going to sleep."

"Don't tell me to shut up, you beast!"

"I just gave you a direct order. Shut your mouth."

Wilma harumphed and began making a smooth spot for herself on the sand. Farouk curled up like a cat right where he was. Wilma lay on the sand and closed her eyes.

"Good night, Farouk," she said.

"Good night, Wilma."

Butler rolled over and closed his eyes. As he drifted off to sleep, he thought he heard faint strains of music on the desert. It was as though the silence of the desert was producing its own subtle sounds, the melody of a flute and the timbre of a lyre, sounds from long ago, of forgotten caravans and mighty sheiks.

21

Butler heard the sound of a small engine. Opening his eyes, he saw that it was light out. The sun was rising in the east and Butler peered over the sand dune in the direction of the engine's sound.

He blinked his eyes because it appeared that coming from his left was a man on a motorcycle. The motorcycle was moving fast and the man was hunched over the handlebars, wearing a black helmet and black one-piece riding suit. The motorcycle and rider whizzed past Butler, not more than thirty yards away, and Butler read the name HONDA on the gas tank. Butler watched in amazement as the motorcycle receded into the shimmering sands of the desert.

Was that a mirage, he wondered, and if so, do mirages make sounds?

"What was that?" Wilma asked, raising her head from the sand.

"A motorcycle," Butler replied.

"A motorcycle?" Farouk asked, still in a ball on the sand.

"That's what I said."

"It couldn't be," Wilma said.

Butler rose from behind the sand dune and walked quickly to where the motorcycle had passed. As he drew closer to the spot he saw black asphalt, and his heart leapt for joy, for it was the road to Damascus. He stomped his feet on it and jumped up and down. It was a real road, and that had been a real motorcycle. Butler had been leading his quarrelsome companions in the right direction, after all. He had been right again.

He returned to the area behind the sand dune, where Farouk and Wilma were getting up and shaking the sand out of their robes.

"It really was a motorcycle," Butler told them. "The road to Damascus is just yonder."

"No kidding?" Wilma asked.

"I wouldn't kid you, baby."

"Well, what do you know about that."

They had a breakfast of protein bars and water, then walked to the road and headed toward Damascus. At around ten o'clock an old green bus came along, and they hailed it down. They got aboard and joined a bunch of peasants with chickens, goats, and sheep. The bus started up and continued on its rickety way toward Damascus. Farouk and Wilma chatted animatedly with the passengers, and Butler pulled his burnoose over his face and fell asleep again. He wasn't that tired, but he wanted an excuse so that he wouldn't have to talk to anybody and reveal that he didn't speak Arabic. That might make people suspicious, and he didn't want people to be suspicious of him while he was carrying so much explosives on his person.

The bus rolled into Damascus at four o'clock in the afternoon and passed a broken-down slum district before reaching the downtown area of modern new hotels and office buildings existing next to ancient mosques and palaces. The sidewalks were thick with people in flowing robes and burnooses. Among them were some men in western dress, and soldiers in khaki.

Butler, Wilma, and Farouk got off the bus at the central terminal and checked into an old hotel nearby. They took baths in a yellowed bathtub down the hall and hid their explosives underneath the mattresses on the beds. After they cleaned up, they returned to the bus terminal and called the Institute from a public telephone. Butler spoke in code to the person who answered, because the Institute wanted no formal connection with the three secret agents, in case the latter got caught. Arrangements were made to meet an official of the Institute at a coffee house not far from the bus station.

The coffee house was on a street corner in a neighborhood of old hotels and garish movie theatres. It had two big windows in front and between them a door that led to the smoky interior where men smoked pipes and drank coffee or tea while playing checkers with each other and talking about the war in Lebanon.

Butler, Farouk, and Wilma sat at a table in the darkest available corner, and when the old mustachioed waiter came over they ordered a pot of coffee and plate of pastries.

The man from the Institute showed up after a short interval, and he wore a white suit with a red carnation in the lapel. He had sandy hair and a thick mustache, and was twenty pounds overweight. They spoke the appropriate code words to each other and then he introduced himself as Harper, the director of the local Institute branch. He sat with them and opened the attaché case he had with him.

"I can't stay long," he said, "because we want to minimize contact between the Institute office and yourselves. However, I think we've got something useful for you." He looked around, and when satisfied he wasn't being observed, he took out a photograph from his attaché case. It showed a thick-set man with blonde hair walking down a street. "This is Dmitri Marakazov, the chief engineer on the Doom Machine project at the Abdul Faheem Munitions Factory. We have been observing him, and he's totally woman-crazy. He'll attempt to have intercourse with any woman from eight to eighty, blind, crippled or crazy. He's forty years old and married, but his wife is in Moscow. This is the first chance he's ever had to mess around, and he's making the most of it."

"But with whom?" Butler asked. "I thought that Arab women don't fool around like that."

"They don't, but there are many western women here,

160

particularly American female tourists. Let's face it, American female tourists can be had."

Wilma wrinkled her nose. "What are you all looking at me for? I'm not a tourist."

"That's true," Butler said. "You're our Mata Hari." He studied the photograph, then turned to Harper. "Does he speak English?"

"Yes, but I understood the lady here speaks Russian."

"I do," Wilma said.

"But I'll assist with the interrogation." Butler said, "and it'll go easier if the sonofabitch speaks English."

"Oh, yes, the interrogation," Harper said. He reached into the attaché case and took out a brown paper bag. "Here's a hypodermic needle and our very latest truth serum. Just give him a shot of this and he'll tell you anything you want to know." Harper snapped closed his attaché case and looked at Butler. "If you have no further questions, I'd better be on my way."

"Do you know when Lover Boy gets out of work?"

"He's on the day shift—usually gets out at five o'clock."

"That's all I need to know," Butler said. "How about you two?"

"I have no questions," Wilma said.

"Me neither," said Farouk.

"Good luck," Harper said. Then he stood and walked out of the coffee house. Seconds later he was swallowed up by the crowd on the sidewalk outside.

Butler turned to Wilma. "It's all up to you now," he said through the smoke and aroma of coffee.

22

It was a quarter to five in the afternoon of the next day. Wilma walked down the street opposite the Abdul Faheem Munitions Factory, wearing blue jeans and denim jacket, her cowboy shirt unbottoned midway down her breasts, taking pictures of the surrounding buildings with her new Canon F-1.

Butler and Farouk were standing nearby, watching her to make sure nothing went wrong. Earlier in the day they'd checked into the kind of hotel where American tourists would stay, with Wilma getting a big room all for herself. They'd shopped for special clothes for Wilma, and bought her the Canon F-1 with three supplemental lenses. She was going to portray an ordinary tourist taking pictures of Damascus, and she was going to bump into Lover Boy by "mistake" and vamp him.

The factory was a huge complex of buildings behind a chain fence, and across the street were cafes, grocery stores, and cheap hotels. It was located near the north of the city, and in the distance you could see the Taurus Mountains.

"Here they come," said Farouk.

Butler looked, seeing men stream out of the buildings toward the main gate. Wilma saw them too and headed in that direction, snapping pictures of the plant, the mountains, and the cafes, just like a shutterbug American tourist. As the workers began filing out of the gate, she started taking pictures of them. Some smiled and waved at her. Others said obscene things. She smiled because she was a tough little cookie and things like that didn't bother her. She kept peering through the reflex system of the camera, searching for the meaty face of Dmitri Marakazov, the Moscow Lover Boy. Somebody pinched her and she went *eek*, but kept on taking pictures. Finally, after several moments had passed, she saw him come through the gate, dressed in baggy gray slacks and a white shirt open at the collar. He carried his suit jacket over his arm.

Wilma made her way toward him, aiming the camera at his face. He spotted her and smiled. She took his picture and then nodded her head as if to say thank you.

"You are American?" he asked, swaggering toward her. He spoke with a thick Russian accent in a deep baritone voice.

"Why, yes," Wilma replied, fluttering her eyelashes. "Are you an Arab?"

"An Arab? Don't be ridiculous. I am a Russian."

"Oh, for goodness sakes. I never met a Russian before."

He laughed heartily at her consternation. "I hope you are not afraid of me."

"Why, no. At least I don't think so. Well, maybe just a little."

He looked her over, and she stuck her breasts out a little. She wore no bra, and didn't have to.

"You are a tourist?" he asked.

"Yes."

"All alone in this strange country?"

"I'm here with some of my girlfriends, but they wanted to go to the Karmlaki Museum today, and I wanted to take pictures of factories. I love factories. I think they're poetic."

"That's probably because you never worked in one," he replied, laughing heartily again. She realized he had a tendency to laugh heartily.

"Probably."

"What do you do for a living?" he asked.

163

"I'm a schoolteacher, and when I get back home I'm going to show color slides of my trip to my students."

"Where are you from?"

"Chattanooga, Tennessee."

"That is in the south of your country?"

"Yes."

"You are in the Ku Klux Klan?"

"No, silly."

"But I thought everybody who lived in the south of your country belonged to the Ku Klux Klan."

"Oh, no. Not anymore."

Dmitri touched his upper lip with his finger and thought for a few seconds. "You are a very attractive young woman," he said.

"Why, thank you," she replied, fluttering her eyelashes.

"Do you think perhaps we could have dinner together?"

"When?"

"Right now."

"Right now?"

"Why not?"

"But I hardly know you."

"What better way would there be for you to know me?" He laughed heartily.

Wilma looked at him and found him utterly disgusting, but the fate of the world hung in the balance there. "Well, all right," she said.

"Is there any particular restaurant where you'd like to go, or should I take you to the Red Star, where all we Russians go to listen to the music of the balalaika."

Wilma wrinkled her nose. "I don't like balalaikas," she said. "Could we go to the Habib?" That was a restaurant where she felt certain she wouldn't get ptomaine poisoning.

"The Habib? I don't believe I know the place."

"It's only a few blocks from my hotel."

"Really?"

"Really."

"Let me get us a cab, and we'll go there right away." He raised his hand and waved.

The street was thick with pedestrians, buses, and automobiles. A cab detached itself from the traffic and steered toward them, stopping a few feet away. Dmitri gallantly opened the door and Wilma scurried inside. Dmitri joined her and told the cabbie the name of the restaurant. The cab moved off into the smoky, honking traffic.

Butler and Farouk came out of the doorway, brushing the dust off their Arabian robes. Butler raised his hand and hailed down a cab. He and Farouk piled in.

"Follow that cab," Farouk told the driver.

"Which cab? There are a hundred cabs out here."

"The one opposite the hydrant, straight ahead."

"Ah, that cab."

And thus Butler and Farouk followed Wilma and Dmitri through the streets of Damascus. They passed the huge Christian church built by Emperor Theodosius I in the year 375 A.D., now known as the Great Mosque of Damascus. They passed steam baths ornate as palaces, office buildings that could have fit on Park Avenue in New York, and the old square buildings built by the French colonials when they governed Syria. Finally they came to the classy downtown area where all the nice hotels were. Wilma's cab stopped in front of the Habib, a modern chromium restaurant, and she got out with Dmitri. They entered the restaurant and then the second cab arrived, disgorging Butler and Farouk.

They looked through the window of the restaurant and saw Dmitri and Wilma being seated at a corner table. Everything seemed to be going okay, but they decided to hang around for awhile anyway before going back to the hotel and waiting for Wilma to arrive with Dmitri. They hunched back and forth on the sidewalk like typical Arabs begging for alms, while inside Wilma and Dmitri dined on roast lamb and couscous, Dmitri made numerous lewd and salacious remarks to Wilma, which she responded to by giggling, though she would have liked to crown the sonofabitch with the bottle of Vichy water that sat on the table.

Finally the meal reached its dessert and coffee stage, and

Butler decided it was time for him and Farouk to return to the hotel and lay their trap for the unfortunate Dmitri. They walked down the sidewalk to the hotel, which was only a few blocks away. Butler hoped that Wilma would be able to handle the big Russian all right. He didn't want anything to happen to her.

In the restaurant, Dmitri's face was flushed from drinking numerous cups of coffee and eating countless slices of baklava. His eyes glittered and he panted like a dog, for Wilma had removed her denim jacket, and now her luxurious breasts could be seen in all their splendor. Dmitri couldn't take his eyes off them, and Wilma wiggled from time to time so he'd stay entranced. Like most women, she'd learned as a teenager to make the most of what she had in order to confuse and befuddle men and thus make them do her bidding.

"You appear to have lost your train of thought," Wilma told him.

He blinked. "Ah, yes. What was I saying?"

"You were saying that Russia is a great country."

"Oh, yes, Russia is a great country. We produce economic miracles there daily. No Russian worker goes without medical care for lack of money, as people do in your country where every doctor is virtually a millionaire because of the fees they charge. Moreover there is no unemployment in the Soviet Union. Everybody has a right to a job, unlike your country, where everybody has to scramble for work, and those that don't find it live in the most squalid poverty. And moreover, there are no slums in the Soviet Union. While it's true that few Russians live as well as many Americans, it's also true that few Russians live as miserably as many Americans, like your blacks and Puerto Ricans and Chicanos, for instance. By the way, may I take you to your hotel room now?"

"My hotel room!" Wilma placed her hand on her breast and looked shocked.

"Why, yes."

"But we hardly know each other!"

"Don't be silly," he said in his deep baritone voice. "Of course we know each other. Why, we've just eaten each other...uh...I mean we've just had dinner together."

"But to my hotel room? What will people think?"

"People don't have to know." He leaned toward her and leered. "Let's end this beautiful evening with the rites of love."

"The rites of love!"

"Yes. You know what I mean." He winked.

She looked at the ceiling. "Well, I don't know." She was trying to drive him insane with lust so that his suspicions would be inhibited.

"Come on, sweetheart," he said, placing his hand on her thigh.

"Gee, do you think we should?"

He moved his hand up her thigh. "I most certainly do."

"But what would my mother think?"

"Your mother won't know."

She took his hand away. "Now stop that!"

"Please let me touch it."

"No!"

"Let me kiss it?"

"Kiss it?!!"

"Yes, kiss it." He rolled his eyes at her.

"Oh, you dirty man," she sighed, fluttering her eyelashes.

"Please let me kiss it."

"I couldn't."

"Why couldn't you?"

"Nobody's ever done that to me before," she lied outrageously.

"Then it's time somebody did, and who would be better to do it for you than a skillful Russian such as myself, a man of the world, an honest worker, and a passionate artist in the rites of love."

"Ooooh," she squealed, wiggling in her seat.

"Let me. Please. For you sake as well as mine." His lips trembled as he grasped her hand.

"Oh, Mr. Dmitri. The things you say!"

"Please," he moaned.

She wondered if his approach actually worked with women. It was the most absurd approach she'd ever seen. "Well," she said, "I don't know if I should."

"Please. I'll die if you don't let me."

"Oh, I wouldn't want you to die, Mr. Dmitri."

"Please."

"All right. If you promise to be good."

"I'll be very good," he said sincerely. "I'll be the best you ever had."

"But I haven't had that many," she lied.

"After me, you won't want any more."

"Oh, Mr. Dmitri. The things you say!"

Dmitri called the waiter over, paid the check, and left a lousy tip. He escorted Wilma out of the restaurant and at the curb the doorman hailed them a cab. They got in and rode the few blocks to the hotel where Wilma's room was.

"Oh, my little *chuchnik*," Dmitri whispered, pawing Wilma in the back seat, pinching her ass and stroking her boobs.

"Now control yourself," she said, fighting him off. "Wait until we get upstairs."

"I can't wait."

"You must."

"I can't. Just let me touch it. Once."

"Touch what?"

"Your little *gridgy*."

"My what?"

"You know. That sweet little thing between your legs."

"Mr. Dmitri!"

"Please, my love."

"Wait. Be patient. We're almost there."

"I can't live without you."

"Sure you can."

"No, I can't."

"It'll only be a few more minutes."

"I can't wait that long."

"Yes you can."

"My blood burns for you."

"Oh, my gosh."

"My heart cries for you."

"Give me a break, will you?"

"Marry me and make me the happiest man in the world."

"But you're already married."

He sat bolt upright and became serious. "How did you know that?"

Wilma knew that she'd made a blunder, and now she had to get out of it. "You mean you're not married?" she asked naively.

"What makes you think I'm married."

"I believe you told me."

"I didn't tell you."

"Then I must have imagined it, because I can't see how a big handsome man like you couldn't be married."

He rolled his eyes. "You think I'm big and handsome, eh?"

"Oh, yes."

"You are in love with me, yes?"

"I don't know. Maybe a little."

"How sweet you are," he crooned. "How charming. How wonderful."

The driver stopped his cab in front of the hotel. "Here we are," he said in Arabic.

Dmitri, who spoke Arabic even worse than he spoke English, paid and tipped him. Then he led Wilma out of the cab and into the hotel. It had a standard lobby that you'd find in an expensive tourist hotel, and resembled the lobby of any big motel in America. Wilma acted shy and demure as Dmitri walked her to the elevator.

"I hope nobody sees us," she whispered to him.

"Why not? We must declare our love to the world!"

"Sssshhhh."

"You Americans are so silly. Soon you will see just how silly you are."

"I am?"

"No, the American people in general."

"Whatever are you talking about, Mr. Dmitri?" she

asked, knowing full well he was making an oblique reference to the terrible Doom Machine.

"Oh, nothing."

"How mysterious you are, Mr. Dmitri."

"Just call me Dmitri. Leave out the mister."

"Okay, Dmitri." She giggled.

The elevator came and they got on with a batch of tourists. They rode up and got off at the tenth floor. Walking down the corridor, Dmitri stroked her behind with one hand, her boobs with the other, and lapped her ears like a dog. At her door, she fumbled with her keys and coughed to alert the boys inside. She hoped they were there and ready for the arrival of Dmitri, because she'd hate to be stuck alone with him in that room.

She opened the door to the darkened hotel room. "After you," she said with a smile.

"No, after you," he replied with a bow.

She giggled and walked into the hotel room. Dmitri followed her, gazing with unblemished lust at her fanny. Suddenly the door slammed closed. Butler and Farouk jumped on Dmitri, and before the poor lovesick Russian knew what was happening, Butler injected the new truth serum into his arm. Dmitri staggered under the weight of the two men as the serum coursed through his body. He fell to his knees and shook his head. I've been betrayed, he thought as he fell over onto his face.

23

Butler and Farouk dragged Dmitri to the bed and tied him to it. Wilma turned on the lights and then went to the bathroom to freshen up. When she returned, Dmitri was knotted to the bed and lying with his eyes closed. Butler and Farouk stood over him on opposite sides of the bed.

"How is he?" Wilma asked.

"Still out," Farouk replied.

"You didn't give him too much of that stuff, did you?"

Butler shook his head. "No." He held the hypodermic needle up to the light. "I gave him the exact perfect amount." He looked at Wilma. "How'd it go?"

"He is a disgusting human being. A complete degenerate. A blob."

Butler snorted sarcastically. "If he looked like Robert Redford you'd think he was the most charming, delightful man that ever lived."

"That's not true! What a nasty, insulting thing to say! And at a crucial time like this, too."

"You're so full of shit."

"How dare you talk to me that way! You're just mad because I wouldn't come across for you once."

"That's not true. I wasn't interested in you at all."

"Liar."

"Nitwit."

"Pig."

"Birdbrain."

Farouk frowned. "You two are driving me crazy. Always insulting each other. I still think you're both in love with each other."

"LOVE!" Butler and Wilma shouted, looking at each other and snarling.

"Yes, love," Farouk said. "I think the best thing you could possibly do would be to go to bed with each other and get it over with, once and for all."

"Go to bed with him?" Wilma asked, making a face. "Are you crazy?"

"Yuk,"Butler said. "It'd be a fate worse than death."

Dmitri groaned, and everybody looked at him. Butler got his pencil and notepad. Dmitri opened his eyes.

"Where am I?" he asked in a faraway voice.

"In my hotel room, lover boy," Wilma replied.

"What happened?"

"Well," Butler said, "things aren't turning out quite the way you expected, old boy. Now if you don't mind, I'd like you to answer a few questions for me. You don't mind, do you?"

Dmitri's face suggested a struggle was going on within him, but he said, "No, I don't mind."

"Good," Butler said. "You are chief engineer on the Doom Machine project, are you not?"

"Doom Machine project?"

"The electronic microwave machine that outsmarts smart bombs."

"Oh, yes, now I know what you're talking about. Yes, I am the chief engineer."

"How soon will the machines be ready?"

"About three more days."

"That's all?"

"That's all."

"Where are the machines being constructed?"

"In the basement of the north wing of the Abdul Faheem Munitions Plant."

"Who is guarding the place where the machines are being constructed?"

"KGB men."

"How many?"

"Six on each shift."

"They work at night?"

"Yes. It's the only part of the plant that is in operation at night."

"Are Russians building the machines?"

"Yes."

"Why not Syrians?"

"It would take too long to teach them the complicated microwave technology."

Butler bent over Dmitri. "Now answer this question very carefully, lover boy. Where are the plans for the machines?"

"The plans?"

"Yes. The blueprints. You know what I mean."

"They are in the project manager's office."

"And where is that?"

"In the basement of the north wing of the Abdul Faheem Munitions Plant."

"Whereabouts in the basement of the north wing of the Abdul Faheem Munitions Plant?"

"It is in the corner of the room. You can't miss it because it is the only office there."

"Is there anyone in that office at night?"

"Yes."

"Who?"

"The person in charge. It could be the foreman, the ranking engineer, or the project manager himself."

"Who is he?"

"Professor Sergei Roussimoff of the Moscow Institute of Science. He is the one who invented Weapon X, which is what we call the machine."

"And where is he right now?"

"How should I know?"

"Where does he live?"

"In the Russian Embassy."

"*In* the Russian Embassy?"

"Correct."

"Why inside the Russian Embassy?" Why doesn't he take an apartment in town?"

"Because he knows how to build Weapon X, and the KGB is afraid he'll be kidnapped."

"Don't you know how to build it, Dmitri?"

"No. I and the others just work from the plans."

"Hmmm. I see." Butler scratched his jaw. "I'm going to have a conference with my friends for a few moments. You just lie here and be quiet, all right, Dmitri?"

"Yes, sir."

Butler motioned with his head to the bathroom; Wilma and Farouk followed him in. He shut the door and they looked at each other in the cramped, humid room. Wilma's cosmetics were atop the sink and a pair of her damp pantyhose hung from the shower nozzle.

"It appears that we don't have as much time as we thought," Butler said. "If the Doom Machine is supposed to go operational in three days, we'll have to act fast. I say we should try to accomplish the mission tonight."

"Tonight?" asked Farouk, looking at his watch. It was eight o'clock.

"Yes," Butler replied. "We'll wait a few hours and then try to break in. The sooner we do this, the better."

"It's okay with me," Wilma said.

"Me too," agreed Farouk.

"Good," said Butler. "Let's get it on."

24

It was midnight in the district where the Abdul Faheem Munitions Plant was located. Three motorcycles sputtered down the deserted streets, and on them were Butler, Farouk, and Wilma. They all wore jeans, denim jackets, and combat boots, for they were completely operational now. The pretense was over. It was do or die. Each carried a gun, a knife, and a tiny camera for taking photographs of the blueprints. They also carried a total of twelve pounds of plastic explosive material, enough to destroy a very large building.

They reached the street facing the plant, and a few of the cafes were open, with a few customers inside. But mostly it was like a ghost town. They saw the front gate of the plant, but it was closed and there were guards in the little building beside it. Driving past the gate, they came to the end of the street and turned left.

This street had the factory on one side and warehouses on the other. They continued to its end and turned left again, driving behind the back of the factory. It had the chain fence around it, and across the street was a vast empty field, for this was the very edge of town. Butler pointed into the field and they drove onto it. He raised his hand and they stopped.

"We'll hide the motorcycles here," he said.

They turned off their motorcycles' engines, dismounted,

and lay the motorcycles behind some bushes. Then they walked out of the field and crossed the street to the sidewalk beside the chain fence.

"You two watch while I cut through the fence," Butler said.

Farouk looked to the right and Wilma to the left as Butler kneeled, took out his laser pen, and burned through the links of the fence on the bottom and two sides. He pushed the fence, and it was like a swinging door hinged on top. Looking both ways, he saw that the coast was clear.

"Let's go in," Butler said.

He kneeled, pushed the fence, and went through. Farouk and Wilma followed him. They ran fifty yards to the wall of the factory and stopped in the shadows, looking and listening.

Everything was quiet.

"Follow me," Butler said.

They moved along the side of the building, staying in the shadows. Finally they came to the kind of window that had opaque glass lined with wire. Its bottom ledge was six feet off the ground.

"Wilma," Butler said, "we'll lift you up, and you burn through the lock with your laser."

"Right," she replied.

Butler grabbed one of her legs and Farouk grabbed the other. They lifted her in the air and she burned through the wood of the window and melted the metal lock that held it. She pushed the sash, and the window opened. The men raised her higher and she went over the ledge into the factory. Butler helped lift Farouk to the ledge, and then he climbed up himself.

The three of them landed on the floor inside the factory. Butler closed the window so no one would notice that they'd come in. They were in a huge dark machine shop, and they could smell grease and scorched metal.

"This way," Butler said.

They crept along the wall of the machine shop, heading in the direction of the north wing of the building. They came to a door—Butler opened it a crack and saw another machine shop.

"Follow me," he said.

They went into the next machine shop, still hugging the wall, looking for a flight of stairs. At the end of the room they found it, and climbed down to the basement.

They found themselves in a huge room filled with gigantic iron cauldrons where chemicals were mixed. Continuing to move in a northerly direction, they made their way through the room.

"Look!" Wilma said, pointing ahead through the legs of the cauldrons.

Butler and Farouk looked, and on the floor ahead in front of the door were the bodies of men. What the hell's going on here? Butler wondered, motioning for Farouk and Wilma to follow him. They crept toward the bodies, and Butler took out his Colt .45. This was the northern wing of the basement, and that must be the room where the Doom Machine is being made, Butler thought. Those bodies on the floor must be the guards, but what had happened to them?

Finally they reached the bodies. There were six of them, and they were unconscious but not dead. Ahead was the door to the Doom Machine project, and it had a window on it. Butler stood stealthily and looked through the window. He saw a room filled with machines and electronic gadgets, and the floor was covered with the bodies of men. At the end of the room was a small office that had a window in its door, and a light shone through the window. Whoever knocked all these people out, Butler thought, is in that room right there.

"Put your hands up!" said a voice in Arabic behind them.

Butler, Farouk, and Wilma raised their hands and looked back. They saw two men in green battle fatigues carrying submachine guns.

"Go in the room," one of the men said.

Butler, Farouk, and Wilma entered the shop where the Doom Machines were being constructed. Butler's heart sank in his chest. They'd been caught, but who the hell caught them? Passing through the room, he noticed that the machinery was ripped apart and burned with acid. Whoever these people were, they had sabotaged the Doom Machine project! And then in a sudden flash Butler realized who they were. He looked behind him to the guns they were carrying, and sure enough, each one of them was carrying an Uzi, the weapon of the Israeli commandos.

"They're Israelis," Butler said.

"Israelis?" asked Farouk.

"Of course!" said Wilma as the truth dawned on her.

Butler turned around and smiled. "Shalom. We are Americans and we come in peace."

"Americans?" asked one of the Israelis.

"Yes."

"CIA?"

"No."

"Who then?"

"Private enterprise."

"Huh?"

The Israeli commandos marched them into the small room, where other Israelis were photographing stacks of blueprints that lay on a table. Tied up and sitting on chairs were some men whom Butler thought were Russian technicians. The Israelis photographing the blueprints looked up at the newcomers. One of them had a long beard and looked like a rabbi. "Who are they?" he asked in Hebrew.

"We're Americans," Wilma replied, because Hebrew was among the repertoire of languages she could speak. "And we come in peace." .

"Americans?" the Israeli asked in English, raising his eyebrows. "CIA?"

"No," Butler said. "We represent a private organization. We've learned of these electronic microwave Doom Machines and have come to destroy them and photograph the blueprints. Our intention was to furnish the blueprints to Israel and the western countries so that the balance of power in the world could be maintained."

"What were you going to destroy the machines with?"

"The plastic explosives that we are carrying on our person."

"And you have cameras with you?"

Butler took out his little spy camera. "Yes."

The Israeli squinted his eyes at Farouk. "Is he an American too?"

"No, he's an Egyptian."

"AN EGYPTIAN!"

The Israelis trained their submachine guns on poor Farouk, whose eyes darted about in fear as he raised his hands in the air.

"But he's a friendly Egyptian," Butler said.

"A truly fine fellow," Wilma added.

"He is working for world peace," Butler said.

"And the brotherhood of man," Wilma added.

"He's practically an American citizen," Butler said.

"Used to teach at the University of North Carolina," Wilma added.

The Israeli said something in Hebrew, and then retreated to a corner of the room for a muted conversation with some of his cohorts, while the others continued photographing the blueprints. After a few minutes the group broke up and the Israeli with the beard advanced toward Butler, Farouk, and Wilma.

"One of you should start photographing the blueprints, and the other two should start placing your explosives, but do so in a manner so that no Syrians get killed. We don't want to make somebody mad at us and start another war. We just want to do what we have to do and get out of here, understand?"

"Gotcha," Butler said.

Butler told Wilma to photograph the blueprints, while he and Farouk went out to the workshop to set the explosives. They made little mounds of plastic and stuck them to the various machines, then attached detonators and strung out their wires. Splicing together the wires, they attached them to a timing device made from Butler's wristwatch. Next they dragged all the drugged bodies out of range of the blast, and finally returned to the office, where Wilma was photographing the blueprints feverishly, and the Israelis were getting ready to leave.

"Can we give you a lift anyplace?" the Israeli commander asked.

"Thanks, but we're not finished yet," Butler replied.

"Well, good luck," the Israeli said.

"Shalom."

"Shalom."

The Israelis turned and left the office. They could be heard running through the workroom of the factory, and then there was silence again. Butler and Farouk took out their cameras and helped Wilma photograph the blueprints. They worked quickly, snapping their shutters and turning over blueprints. The tension was building; they knew that the longer they were in the factory, the more vulnerable they would be. Finally the last blueprint was photographed, and they put away their cameras.

"Let's get the hell out of here," Butler said.

They left the office, and in the workshop Butler set the timing device to go off in fifteen minutes. Then they left the workshop and entered the room that held the gigantic vats, moving quickly among them and up the stairs to the machine shop. They crept along the wall and climbed out the window. Running toward the fence, they pushed through the opening and crossed the street. They found their motorcycles in the bushes on the other side. Starting up their motorcycles, they roared away.

A few blocks later, as they were passing a mosque, they heard the explosions. They weren't very loud, and turning around, they could see nothing, because there wasn't that much explosive material involved. Just enough to destroy the Doom Machine project.

But their mission wasn't over yet. They still had to get their film to the Institute. They headed in that direction, intending to drop the film off with whoever was on duty, but they began to hear the sirens. The Syrian constabulary finally realized that something was amiss in the Abdul Faheem Munitions Plant.

The sound of sirens grew louder, and in the distance down the long boulevard they could see swarms of headlights.

"We'd better ditch these motorcycles," Butler said.

They drove toward the curb, went over it, turned off their engines, and pushed the motorcycles into an alley. They waited, and soon a convoy of military trucks and jeeps went speeding by on its way to the factory. The trucks were loaded with soldiers wearing helmets and carrying rifles.

"I think we ought to leave the motorcycles here and go on foot the rest of the way," Butler said.

Wilma shook her head. "We can get there faster if we take the motorcycles."

"But they'll have roadblocks and they'll stop the motorcycles. If we're on foot it'll be harder for them to see us."

Farouk shook his head. "If we go on foot we might never get there. I think Wilma is right."

Butler wished he had a cigarette. "I think you're both wrong."

"It's two against one," Wilma said.

"This mission is not a democracy," Butler replied. "I'm in charge here, and I say we go on foot."

"Brute," Wilma said.

"Dictator," Farouk added.

"Get off your motorcycles and let's go," Butler ordered.

They dismounted and Butler led them through the alley to the next street, which was lined with white stucco homes. They continued walking, and on the next block came to a series of stores closed for the night. One of the stores sold clothes, and Butler got an idea.

"I think we'd better break in here and get some authentic native garb," he said, taking out his laser pen.

He burned through the lock and they entered the dark store. Piles of clothes were stacked on tables. Butler selected a brown robe with black burnoose, Wilma dressed in white,

181

and Farouk chose green. They put the clothes on and soon they looked like three traditional Arabs.

"Okay," Butler said. "This is what we're going to do now. It'll look very suspicious to be out on the streets tonight, so I think we'd better check into the nearest hotel and go to the institute in the morning."

"How are we going to do that?" Farouk asked. "The Arabs will frown on two men and one woman checking into the same hotel room."

"So we'll separate and take private rooms."

"How are you going to check into a hotel if you don't speak Arabic?" Wilma asked Butler.

"That's right too," Butler replied. "That means I'll have to check in with Farouk."

Farouk shook his head. "No good, because that'll mean Wilma will have to take a room all by herself, and that will look very suspicious. They'll think she's a prostitute and she'll probably be arrested. No, someone will have to share a room with Wilma."

Butler pointed at Farouk. "You share the room with Wilma."

Farouk looked exasperated. "Then how are you going to get a room, since you don't speak Arabic?"

"That's right too," Butler said.

"The inescapable solution," Farouk continued, "will be for you to share the room with Wilma."

"Oh, shit," Wilma said.

"There must be another way," Butler said.

"No," Farouk replied. "There is no other way. Think about it."

Butler thought about it. "You're right."

"Oh, shit," Wilma said.

Butler squared his shoulders. "Well, I suppose we have to do what's best for the mission. Wilma and I will get a room together in one hotel, and you will check into another hotel. In the morning we'll go to the Institute separately, you alone Farouk, and me with Wilma. And to make sure the film gets there, I think I'd better carry it all, just in case."

182

Wilma looked at him haughtily. "What makes you think you have a better chance than us of getting through."

"Because I'm more experienced at this stuff. Now hand over the film and shut up."

Farouk and Wilma reached under their robes and removed handfuls of the tiny film cartridges which they gave Butler. He put them in the pockets of his jeans.

"We might as well split up now," Butler said. "You go first, Farouk. Check into the first hotel you see, and in the morning go directly to the Institute. Got it?"

"I've got it."

"So long, and good luck." Butler patted him on the shoulder.

Wilma kissed his cheek. "Good luck, Farouk."

"Good luck to the both of you," Farouk replied. Then, covering his face with the robe, he walked to the door of the shop, where he paused, listened, and then slipped out into the street. Butler stood in the shadows near the front window and watched Farouk walk along the sidewalk, his shoulders hunched over, a typical Arab to anyone who didn't know better. Butler waited a few minutes, then turned to Wilma.

"Let's go," he said.

She pointed her finger at him. "Listen you—I want to get something straight with you right here and now. There's not going to be any funny business between us, understand?"

He snorted. "I'm a professional, and I don't have time for funny business. Now let's go."

He opened the door and they left the clothing shop. They walked down the dark street to the corner and then turned east toward the direction of the Institute. A convoy of three armored personnel carriers passed, speeding toward the factory, and Butler huddled next to Wilma.

After a few blocks they entered the Casbah district of Damascus. There were cafes and restaurants still open, and a number of non-Arabs prowling the streets. Policemen stood on the street corners, and Butler tried to pretend that he was a humble, ignorant man.

Next to a movie theatre showing a French film they found

183

a seedy five-story hotel. They stood outside and looked into its lobby.

"I guess this one's as good as any," Butler mumbled into her ear. "Let's go."

"But it looks nasty in there."

"We don't have much choice, because we have to get off the streets."

"Isn't that a hotel there on the next block? See the sign?"

"I can't read Arabic, remember?"

"Let's try that one."

"I said, let's go in this one."

"You're a tyrant, do you know that?"

"I'm just the commander of this mission," he replied. "I am the General and you are the Private, so let's go."

"I hate you," she hissed.

"Kiss my ass. What in the hell do I care what you hate, you silly little bitch."

She narrowed her eyes. "Someday you're going to pay for that remark."

"Shut up and let's check into this damned hotel, you pain in the ass."

He took her arm and together they walked into the hotel lobby. A few Arabs were sprawled on dilapidated sofas, huge circular fans turned lazily overhead, and behind the counter was another Arab in a fez, resting on his elbows and reading a newspaper. He had a long mustache and a nose like a banana.

Wilma bowed to him like a shy peasant woman. "My husband I would like to have a room for the night, sir," she said in Arabic.

"Hmmmmm," he said, looking them over. "Hmmmm. Where are you folks from?"

"Aleppo. We've come seeking work."

The Arab looked at Butler. "What kind of work do you do?"

Butler stared at him and began to turn green.

Wilma pointed her finger in the air. "My husband has

taken a vow of silence to Allah," she said. "He will not speak until Israel is destroyed."

The Arab shook his head. "That was not a very smart vow. Israel probably never will be destroyed. Your husband may never speak again. Perhaps he should reconsider."

"Oh, no, sir. He feels very strongly about it. He hates the Israelis with all his heart and soul."

"He's a good man," the Arab said, saluting Butler.

Butler smiled and saluted back, although he didn't know what was going on.

Wilma signed the register, paid the man, and accepted the key to the room. She took Butler's arm and they climbed the stairs to the third floor, walked down the murky corridor, and stopped at the door of a hotel room. She inserted the key in the lock and they entered the room. He closed the door and bolted it, while she flicked the light switch near the door. A lamp beside the bed went on. The bed wasn't very wide and sagged in the middle. It was covered with a motheaten blanket and had two pillows. The window was open and the sounds of the street could be heard. Adjacent to the room was a tiny bathroom with a sink, commode, and bathtub with a dirty ring around it.

"What a joint!" Butler said.

Wilma removed her shawl, revealing her gleaming black hair. "It's only for a night. Mind if I use the toilet first?"

"Go ahead."

She went in the bathroom and closed the door, and he walked to the window and looked down. A cafe was across the street and men in white suits sat at outdoor tables playing dominoes and drinking tea out of glasses. From afar a woman was singing an Arabic song, and the sound was mournful.

Wilma came out of the bathroom, the sound of the toilet flushing behind her. "Your turn," she said.

Butler went into the bathroom, took a leak, and washed his face and hands. Now that the pressure was momentarily off, he was aware of his jangled nerves and the unpleasant

185

throbbing sensation underneath his temples. When this operation was over he was going to take a long vacation. Maybe he'd go to Cairo and see the pyramids, King Tut's tomb, and the other relics of that old and distinguished civilization. And then perhaps he'd go to Alexandria to see if it really was the way Lawrence Durrell described it in his books, with exotic depraved women everywhere. Yes, that was a good idea. The Institute owed him some back pay and he'd blow it all in Alexandria. What the hell.

He returned to the hotel room and saw Wilma lying on the bed with her clothes on.

"What the hell are you doing with your clothes on?" he asked.

"Wearing them," she replied.

"Take them off."

"WHAT!"

"You heard me. These hotels are full of police spies. What will they think if they come in here and find a husband and wife in bed with their clothes on. They'll know something's fishy immediately and drag us both down to the nearest police station, where they'll find the film and all the other goodies, and we'll never be heard from again."

"You're just making all that up for low, sexual reasons," she said in an accusing, condescending voice.

"I am not."

"You are too."

He pointed his finger at her. "Listen here, you little twirp. What makes you think I want to see your funny little body. I'm interested solely in the safety of our mission. Don't forget—the fate of the world is in the balance here."

"The Israelis have the damned Doom Machine plans. They'll give it to America and the other Western countries."

"Maybe, and maybe not. Who knows what will happen tomorrow? We've got to follow through on our mission. Now take your clothes off and get under the covers. I'll look the other way, since you're so concerned about your ridiculous little body being seen by me."

"Is that a direct order?" she asked.

186

"You're damned right it is."

She looked at him with hate in her eyes. "I'll never go out on another operation with you, no matter what it is."

"I wouldn't let you. You're a little pain in the ass. No, I take it back. You're a *big* pain in the ass."

"Harumph," she said, raising her nose in the air. "Turn around."

He turned around and heard her rise from the bed and start undressing. He heard cloth gliding against cloth and garments falling to the floor. He chuckled to himself because she was right—he did have ulterior motives of the lowest sort. He felt certain that if he could get into bed naked with her, he could screw her. She was a woman, after all, and she had normal feelings. She wouldn't be able to resist him.

"Can I leave my underclothes on?" she asked.

"Of course not. Arab women don't wear underwear from fancy American department stores."

"I get mine in Paris," she said.

"Take them off, nitwit."

"You know," she said, "you really do make me sick."

"Shut up and hurry up. I want to go to bed."

He heard the sound of silk against skin, and imagined her underpants coming down. It occurred to him that it was the most beautiful and subtle sound in the world, a bit like music, actually. He heard her get into bed, the springs creaking.

"You can turn around now," she said.

He turned and saw her in bed, covered up to her chin. He also saw that when he joined her they'd have to touch, because the bed was that narrow. Snorting in anticipation of fun and games, he took off his burnoose. She rolled the other way so she couldn't see.

"You can look—I don't give a damn," Butler said, pulling off his robe.

"Yuk. Who wants to look at you?"

"If you didn't care, it wouldn't matter to you at all."

"It doesn't matter to me at all."

"Then why don't you just look?"

"Oh, shut up and get undressed."

"Are you afraid that you'll see something that you'll like?"

"You don't have anything that I like, Mr. Butler. Get that through your head right now."

Chuckling to himself, Butler undressed. He gathered together his American clothes and Wilma's and hid them under the mattress on his side of the bed, in case there was a search. The exposed film also went under the mattress. He put his Colt .45 under the pillow, while she lay still with her eyes closed shut.

"I'm coming to bed now," he said.

"Who cares?"

He turned off the lamp and crawled under the covers with her. It was warm and smelled like jasmine flowers. His pelvic bone touched her ass, and she twitched.

"Stay away from me," she said in a deadly voice.

"I'm trying to, but the bed's so small and there's this indentation in the middle that draws us together, as it were."

"You're doing it on purpose."

"I am not."

"You are too."

Butler lay still on his back, feeling her ass against his hip. She was a pretty little wench and she had a great figure, so naturally an erection began to grow between his legs. Now that they were hidden and there was no imminent danger, his mind was free to sink to its normal state of utter depravity. He thought of her delicious body and how wonderful it would be to lie between her supple legs. He imagined that her nipples would taste like raspberries and her lips like honey.

He decided that the time had come for him to make his move. Turning toward her, he pressed his cock against the crack of her fanny.

She leapt two feet in the air and scrambled to the edge of her mattress. "Stop that!"

He came after her and touched her with it again. "Stop what?"

"You have a . . . an erection!"

"Why, so I do."

"Get rid of it this instant!" she screamed, shivering at the edge of the bed.

"How am I going to get rid of it?" he cooed.

"I don't know," she snapped. "That's your problem."

There was the sound of footsteps in the corridor.

"Uh-oh, police spies," Butler said. "C'mere."

He hugged her to him and she struggled to get away.

"Ssshhh," he whispered in her ear. "If they peek in here we have to make like we're married."

Sure enough, a key turned in the lock. They lay side by side with his penis against her belly, and he noticed that she was breathing hard. The door opened, some men mumbled in Arabic, then it closed and was locked again.

He continued to hold her tightly. "They might come back."

"Please let me go," she whimpered.

"I don't dare let you go. What if they come in here again?"

"I can hear them walking away."

"I can't," he lied.

"Well I can. Get away from me, damnit."

"Are you sure it's safe?"

"Yes, I'm sure it's safe."

"We can't take chances, you know."

"I know."

"It's better to be safe than sorry."

"Let me go."

"They taught us in the CIA that you never can take enough precautions."

"You're taking advantage of me, you beast."

"How?"

"You're trying to make me horny so that I'll do piggy things with you."

"I am not. I'm only trying to be a good, cautious agent."

"Take that thing away from me or I'll pinch it."

"Go ahead and pinch it."

"If I do they'll hear you all the way to Tel Aviv."

"I don't care."

"Get away from me!"

189

"No."

"I'm getting out of this bed right now. I don't care what happens—I can't take it any more."

She turned away from him and tried to get out of bed, but he grabbed her by the waist and pulled her back to him. She was bent over as she rolled into bed and he jabbed his shaft between her legs from behind. His aim was perfect, and she went limp in his arms. her fanny thrust out against him.

"You're wearing me down," she said.

"You feel awfully nice down there," he replied.

"You're a bastard."

"But lovable."

"No, not lovable."

He swiveled his hips, rubbing the shank of his penis through her valley of love.

"I hate you," she sighed.

"If you hate me, how come you're so juicy down there?"

"Let me go."

He held her tighter. "No."

"Please?"

"No."

"I beg you."

"No."

"You're an animal, Butler," she said in a weakening voice. "If we ever get out of this I'm going to shoot you right between the legs."

"How come you're so juicy down there, sweetheart?" he asked, reaching around and touching her with his finger.

"You're despicable. You're taking advantage of me."

"How come you're so juicy down there?"

"Please don't," she whimpered.

"Answer my question," he demanded.

"Because you're taking advantage of me."

"How am I taking advantage of you?"

"Because I'm only a woman and you're stimulating me in a most cruel and lascivious way."

"But is it really cruel?" he asked, finding the hot spot and sticking his cock in an inch.

"Yes," she sighed.

He jabbed in another inch. "Am I really hurting you that badly? Because if I am I'll take it out."

"You couldn't take it out now," she moaned.

"Oh, yes I could."

"You don't have the willpower."

"Oh, yes I do."

"You do not."

"Then watch, or I should say, feel."

Slowly he began to withdraw from her.

"No—stop!" she cried.

"What's wrong?"

"Nothing's wrong."

"You don't want me to take it out?"

"Yes, I want you to take it out."

"Then why did you tell me to stop when I was taking it out?"

"I don't know," she said, trembling in his arms.

"I know," he replied, kissing her ear.

"Explain it to me," she whispered.

"Because I've got you all hot and bothered now, and you want to do it with me. Right?"

"Stop tormenting me, please."

"How am I tormenting you?"

"By raping me."

"I'm not raping you!" he said indignantly, pushing in another inch.

"You are too," she replied, pushing her backside against him, drawing him in deeper.

"This isn't rape—it's seduction," he insisted.

"Seduction? Don't make me laugh. We are forced to be in bed together, and you have taken advantage of my femininity and weakness like the beast that you are."

He pushed her onto her stomach and inserted himself into her all the way as she spread her legs for him. They sighed together. He cupped her breasts and kissed her neck. She rocked her hips back and forth.

"Oooohhhh," she said.

"Aaaahhhhh," he replied.

He began to work her slowly, moving all the way in and all the way out, holding her breasts tightly, and licking her ears. She wiggled underneath him, thrusting her bottom at him rhythmically, and clawing at the pillow.

"You're a very good lover," she whispered. "You're a beast and a cad, and you're not very smart, but you're a very good lover."

"You're a bitch and a pain in the ass, but you've got the loveliest, sexiest body in the world."

"Oh, come on. I'll bet you say that to all the girls."

"I do."

"You bastard."

He chortled as he changed his position and thus altered his angle of entry.

"What did you just do?" she asked, dazed.

"Moved a little."

"You just made me see stars."

"Really?"

"And they were in Technicolor."

"How nice."

"Oh, you're good, Butler."

"I'll bet you say that to all the guys too."

"Not all of them. Oh, and you're so big, Butler."

"I bet you say that to all the guys too."

"No, you're really big. I can feel you deep inside me."

"What does it feel like?" He reached down with both his hands and tenderly caressed the lips of her vagina with his fingertips.

"Oh, my goodness, what are you doing to me?" she asked.

"What does it feel like?"

"You're making me dizzy. You're going to make me come."

"Good. I want you to come and completely freak out."

"You beast."

He quickened his motion. "Come on—come."

"I can't stand it any more. I'm going to lose my mind," she breathed.

"You can't lose anything that you don't have."

"I'm afraid," she said with a tremble.

"Don't be afraid."

"I'm afraid I'll get so far out that I'll never come back again."

"I'll make sure you come back again, becuase I want you to blow me."

"You bastard."

"You'll love it."

"You're just talking dirty because you know it turns me on even more."

"You've got the sweetest pussy in the world, kid."

"You're rotten, Butler."

"Come for me."

"I won't."

"Please?"

"No."

"Yes."

"Oh. Oh. Oooohhh."

"More."

"OOOOHHHHHHH."

She bucked like a bronco and thrashed her head against the pillow while he drilled her with all his might. His fingers twiddled her vagina while his cock rammed in again. He fucked her energetically, almost savagely, pushing her small body down on the bed again and again. Tears ran down her eyes and she bit her lower lip.

"Oh," she said. "Oh, oh, oh, OOOOHHHHHHHH!"

"Come more," he coaxed.

"Ay, ay, ay, AAAAAYYYYYYYYYYYY!"

"More."

"I can't," she gasped.

"Yes you can."

"Please don't."

"Come more."

"Oh, Butler. Oh. Ah ay oh eeeeeeeeeeee."

"More."

He grabbed her by her hair and pulled her down against

his rampaging cock. She flailed her arms and legs, and saliva oozed from a corner of her mouth. She no longer was a proper lady with a degree from Radcliffe and an impressive career as an undercover agent. She was a sex-maddened female creature in the throes of the most powerful orgasm in her life.

"AAAAAIIIIIIIIIIIEEEEEEEEEEEE!"

Gradually her motions lost their fervor, as she gasped for air. Her body dripped with perspiration and her jaw hung open. Noticing this, Butler slowed down also. Then they became still, he lying on top of her, his cock still deep inside her, and she still on her tummy.

"Oh," she sighed.

Butler was breathing hard, his face burrowed in her hair that furled around her neck. He moved his hands down and held his palms against her smooth belly.

"You're a regular little tiger, aren't you?" he asked throatily.

"Oh, Butler, what you do to me!" she sighed.

"You liked it, didn't you."

"I loved it."

"You came so beautifully."

"What did I come like?"

"Like dawn."

"Oh, Butler, that's such a sweet thing to say."

"You're an angel."

"You're a fabulous lover, Butler."

"Only because you inspired me so."

"That's also a sweet thing to say. I never realized you could be so nice."

"And it's not over yet either."

She went stiff underneath him. "What do you mean—it's not over yet."

"We have only just begun, my dear."

She shook her head in firm little motions. "No Butler, I couldn't."

"Yes you can."

"No, I don't have any more strength."

"Yes you do."

"I'll lose my mind if you keep doing this to me."

"It won't be any great loss to the world."

"Don't, Butler."

"I'm sorry, but I'm not finished with you yet."

"Please."

"Save your breath."

As they spoke, he pulled his cock out of her and rolled her over onto her back. She hugged her legs tightly together and crossed her arms over her breasts.

"I'm not going to let you," she said, looking up at him with doe eyes.

"Yes you will," he replied, kneeling beside her.

"I won't."

"Oh yes you will."

"You'll have to rape me."

"No I won't."

"You'll have to knock me unconscious."

"Don't be ridiculous," he said with a smile as he lowered his head and kissed the little muff at the juncture of her legs.

"Oh, you're not going to do *that*, are you?" she asked, alarmed.

"Ain't I?"

"That's not fair, Butler."

"Sssshhhhh."

"Stop it."

"I can't."

She raised her hands and tried to push his shaggy head away, but he merely took her wrists and pinned them to the mattress.

"Please let me go, Butler," she whimpered. "I don't want you to make me crazy again."

He ran his tongue through her juicy little slit.

"Now you're really taking advantage," she said.

"Stop complaining so much. There are thousands of women who'd give all they had to trade places with you right now."

"I like to be normal and rational," she whined. "I don't like to go crazy."

"Yes you do."

"No I don't."

"You mean you didn't enjoy that before."

"I did, but I don't want any more. Enough is enough. Know what I mean?"

"No." He found her clitty and kissed it.

"Stop that," she said weakly.

"Never."

"Please?"

"Sorry, but no dice."

"Bastard."

"Open your legs."

"No."

"Then I'll have to make you, won't I?"

"Stop it!"

She squirmed and tried to get away, but he held her wrists tightly.

"You're trying to destroy me," she said with a sob.

"No I'm not," he murmured into her bush.

"God is going to punish you for what you're doing to me."

"I'm not a very religious man."

"Oooohhhh."

"Open your legs."

"Aaaahhhhh."

"Come on."

"Please don't."

She wasn't trying to get away anymore, so he let her wrists loose and cupped her ass in his hands.

"I'm losing control of myself again," she said from somewhere at the bottom of her throat.

"Good."

"I'm going to go bananas."

"Go ahead."

"It'll be the end of me."

"Open your legs."

"No."

"Go ahead." He nibbled her clitoris with his teeth.

"Ooohhhh," she sighed as she let her legs open.

"More."

"Ohhhh."

"More, I said." He thrust his tongue deep inside her.

"OH!"

He moved his tongue in and out of her, tasting her beautiful essence, feeling her most hidden secrets.

"Oooohhhhh," she moaned, opening her legs wider.

He kissed her again, then crawled up her body, licking her bellybutton, sucking her breasts, and fastening his teeth on her throat as he slid his cock into her.

"Ahhhhh," she moaned as it went in all the way. "I think I've died and gone to heaven."

"So have I."

"But I don't want you to think I'm in love with you or anything like that."

"Of course not."

"I just can't help myself."

"I quite understand."

"I'm going to hate you in the morning."

"Hate me in the morning, but love me tonight. That's my motto."

"You're disgusting."

"You're delicious."

"Oh, you beast."

"Stop calling me that. I'm a man."

"You're not a man. You're an animal. A raging creature from the black lagoon."

"What a fantasy that is."

"It's the truth."

"It's the fantasy that turns you on."

She swiveled her hips a little. "it's gotten bigger, do you know that?"

"It has not."

"Yes it has. I can feel it. It's bigger. Much bigger."

"How much bigger."

"Twelve inches bigger."

"That's impossible. It wasn't twelve inches in the first place."

"Yes it was. And now it feels like it's up to my throat."

He laughed.

"It feels so good," she whispered. "It's splitting me in half."

"Should I take it out now?"

"Don't you dare!"

"But I thought you didn't want to do this."

"That was before. I've changed my mind."

"Why?"

"I don't know why. Fuck me, Butler, and stop talking."

She groaned as Butler backed off, and sighed as he eased in again.

"Did you like that?" he asked.

"You know I did."

"Want me to do it again?"

"If you don't I'll kill you."

He drew back again, then buried himself deep into her. He lay still and let it soak.

"More," she uttered.

"Hungry little bitch, aren't you?"

"You're destroying my soul, Butler. You're turning me into a sex degenerate."

"You were a sex degenerate long before you ever met me."

"That's not true."

"The first time I ever set eyes on you I knew you were a hot little number."

"How did you know?"

"I didn't know, but I could tell."

"Did I look a certain way?"

"Yes."

"How?"

"Like the kind of woman who could fuck for days."

"I couldn't fuck for days."

"Oh yes you could. I'd like to get you alone in a house someplace with enough food and drink so that we wouldn't have to go out, and we'd fuck all the time. I'd hide your clothes so that you couldn't get dressed."

"Oh, Butler, let's do it sometime."

"Do you really want to?"

"I do—I do."

"When we get out of here, you'll change your mind."

"No I won't."

"You'll start to play the proper little lady again."

"I could never be that way with you again."

"Bullshit."

"I couldn't."

"Bullshit."

"You don't believe me?"

"No."

"I'll prove it to you—you'll see."

"I don't believe you, but right now I'm going to prove something to you."

Butler began pumping her slowly, moving all the way in and all the way out, holding her by the waist. She gripped him by the shoulders, raising her knees up, meeting him stroke for stroke.

"Oh, that's so good," she whispered.

"Your body is perfect—just the right size."

"Oh," she said. "Oh."

"Ah."

They kissed and touched tongues, the warm breath from their nostrils rushing against each other. She moved her hands down and gripped the cheeks of his ass, and he held her waist, increasing his tempo.

"It's getting bigger," she sighed.

"You're dreaming."

"It is—it is."

"I wish I had another one and four more hands, because I want to do more to you."

"You're insatiable, you beast."

"You make me that way."

"Where did you learn to do it like this?" she inquired.

"You're teaching me right now."

"Oh, Butler."

She bounced about on the bed, scratching his back,

breathing hard into his ear. Wrapping her legs around him, she tightened her vaginal muscles around his cock and milked it down.

"Oh," he said, his eyes rolling up into his head.

"What's the matter?"

"Don't do what, Wilma."

"Why not?"

"The pleasure—the sensation—it's just more than I can bear."

"Aha!" she said, her eyes lighting up. "Now I've got you where I want you, you dog."

"Don't Wilma!"

"Beg, you swine!"

"Please don't!"

She laughed and squeezed his dick with her vaginal muscles as she rocked against him. Butler felt the world spinning around him, his knees became jelly and his lips trembled. He'd wanted to keep screwing her until she passed out so she'd know who was boss, but now she'd turned the tables and he was afraid he'd start screaming, for the ecstasy was that intense. There was a maddening itch in his testicles, and he knew what that meant. It meant he was going to come, and he didn't want to come yet.

"Stop it!"

But she held him tighter and worked him more vigorously. His balls exploded and he went into convulsions as the hot cream burst out of him. Still she held onto him like a little monkey, milking him dry with her vaginal muscles. He moaned and stuttered. He drove deep and hard into her while at the same time he tried to get away. He didn't know who he was or where he was. He was weak as a kitten and mighty as a lion.

She turned him loose and pushed him off her. He fell onto his back, and dazedly wondered what do to next, when she fell on him and stuffed his oozing penis into her mouth. She held its root with her little fist and pressed the palm of her other hand against his quivering stomach as she sucked him off. She nibbled its head and then pushed it deep into her throat. He reached around and put his four fingers into her steaming hole.

She moved her lips up and down his cock and sucked him dry. Then, when they were exhausted totally, they collapsed into each other's arms and fell immediately into a deep, dreamless sleep.

25

Butler opened his eyes and saw sunlight streaming through the ragged curtains of the hotel room. He looked at his watch and saw only a blank stretch of his wrist. Then he remembered that he'd used his watch to set off the explosions in the Abdul Faheem Munitions Plant, and that there was film underneath the mattress that he had to get to the nearest Institute office without delay.

He rolled over and saw Wilma B. Willoughby looking at him.

"Bastard," she said.

"Get your clothes on. We've got to get going."

"I hope you don't think I'm in love with you or anything like that because of what happened last night."

"Shut your yap and get your clothes on."

They rolled out of the creaking bed that was creaking a lot worse this morning than it was last night. Wilma stretched and yawned while Butler fetched their clothes and the film from under the mattress. They dressed, putting on their American clothes first and the Arab robes last. Butler stored the film cassettes in his pants pockets and jabbed his Colt .45 into his belt. He put on his burnoose and folded the material so that it covered most of his face.

"You ready?" Butler asked.

She was standing in front of the mirror, adjusting the veil over her face. "In a minute."

"Hurry up."

She looked at herself in the mirror and frowned. Whenever she screwed all night she looked like hell in the morning. That was one of the reasons she hated to screw all night.

"I'm ready," she said.

"Let's go."

They left the room, walked down the corridor, and descended the stairs. The lobby was brighter in daylight, but not much. Arab men sat around reading newspapers and the same clerk was behind the counter.

"You sleep well?" he asked.

"Yes," replied Wilma.

"Have you heard what happened last night?"

"What?"

"Israeli spies set off explosions in the Abdul Faheem Munitions Factory. It was a cowardly act, so typical of them."

"The dogs."

"But we'll catch them—don't worry about it."

"Of course we'll catch them."

"In fact, we've probably already caught them."

"Probably."

Butler and Wilma left the hotel and walked out of the Casbah to the downtown area where the Institute maintained its offices in one of the modern new buildings. They passed parks, bazaars, and squads of armed soldiers on street corners, but they kept moving along, a humble Arab couple. The sun was shining as they crossed a public square and came upon a man sitting on a blanket selling oranges. Wilma bought two, gave one to Butler, and they continued on their way, sucking oranges.

Finally they reached the downtown area. The streets were congested with buses, taxis, and private cars. Businessmen raced along the sidewalks with briefcases in hand, while in the shadows humble peasants were slunking along, dreaming of date trees and Allah. The building where the Institute had its offices was one of the largest in Damascus, just down

203

the street from the fashionable Fawzi Hotel.

Butler and Wilma entered the building and walked to the elevator. Businessmen looked at them, wondering what the peasants were doing in the fancy building. They got on the elevator and rode up to the twenty-fifth floor, where the Institute's offices were. They got off the elevator and entered the reception room of the Institute.

An Arab receptionist sitting behind the desk looked up at them and smiled. "May I help you?" she asked in Arabic.

"We'd like to see Mr. Harper, please."

The receptionist looked at them and narrowed her eyes. "Butler and Willoughby?"

They nodded.

"He's expecting you. I'll take you back to him."

She got up and led them down the twisting corridors lined with offices, where Institute employees looked with curiosity at the strange Arab couple. Finally they came to the corner office of the director. The receptionist muttered a few words to the secretary, then Butler and Wilma were invited to enter the office.

Butler opened the door and motioned for Wilma to go first. They went inside, and sitting behind the desk was Harper in a gray suit with white shirt and black tie. Farouk was sitting in a chair against the wall, smoking an Egyptian cigarette.

Harper arose and smiled. "I'm so glad you made it. We were getting worried about you."

"What time is it?" Butler asked.

"One o'clock in the afternoon. What took you so long?"

Butler looked at Wilma and tried to think fast. "We decided to leave later when the streets were more crowded, to avoid detection."

"You have the film with you?"

"Yes." Butler lifted his robes and emptied his pockets onto the desk.

Harper scooped up the tiny film cassettes and looked at them as though he had a handful of jewels. "I'll have these developed right away, and then we'll transmit the wirephotos to Headquarters. Stay here—I'll be right back."

Harper walked quickly out of the office, while Butler and Wilma dropped into chairs in front of the desk.

"You got a cigarette?" Butler asked Farouk.

"Here," Farouk replied, holding out his pack.

Butler took a cigarette and accepted a light from Farouk. He inhaled deeply, got a little dizzy, and blew out the smoke.

"You have any trouble getting back?" Butler asked him.

"There were a lot of police and soldiers, but none of them stopped me."

"That's about the way it was with us."

Farouk leered at them. "Did you two sleep well?"

"Terrible," Butler said.

"Awful," Wilma agreed.

Farouk snorted. "I bet."

Wilma's eyes shot sparks. "What do you mean by that?"

"Nothing."

"You don't think that I'd let this sonofabitch animal touch me, do you?"

"Of course not."

"Well, I didn't."

"Are you sure?"

"I DIDN'T, DAMNIT!"

"Okay, okay," Farouk said. "Don't get mad."

Harper returned to the office, smiling jovially. "Good work, all of you," he said as he sat behind his desk. "Those photos will be in Big Sur in about an hour or so, and I've just transmitted a brief message to let them know that your mission was accomplished. It was a most difficult mission and I don't mind admitting that I had my doubts that you could bring it off, but you did. I am most impressed. Of course we have to admit that perhaps the mission wasn't as necessary as we thought it was, since the Israelis obtained the Doom Machine plans on their own, and doubtless would have made them available to the United States, for they have a reciprocal spy agreement. But anyway, you did it, and masterfully, if you don't mind me saying so." Harper glanced at his watch. "Well, I imagine you're all anxious to get out of here. We'll fix you up with appropriate clothing and papers, and you can all leave on one of the evening flights. You'll be back in California before you know it."

"Marvelous," Butler replied, puffing his cigarette. "I can't wait to get back to California.

"I can," Wilma said snootily. "I think I'll stick around Damascus for awhile and then leave on a later flight."

"I think I will too," Farouk said.

Harper looked surprised. "How about you, Butler? Do you want to stick around too?"

"Hell, no. I want to get out of here as quickly as I can."

"Good. Well, that's all. I'll have my staff make all the travel arrangements."

Wilma leaned forward in her chair. "There's one more thing."

"What's that?" Harper asked.

"I'd like you to mention in your report that I don't want to be assigned to a mission with Mr. Butler ever again."

Harper frowned. "I see. Well. I'll mention that of course, if you want me to, but you'll have to make your own request to our personnel department."

"You can be sure I'll do that," Wilma replied, giving Butler a dirty look. She stood up. "Well, if there's nothing further to discuss, I think I'll be going. I assume the Institute will have quarters for me someplace?"

"Speak to my secretary."

Farouk stood. "I think I'll be going too."

Harper rose and shook their hands. "Well, good luck, and my congratulations again."

"Thank you."

Farouk shook hands formally with Butler, then Farouk and Wilma left the office. Wilma didn't look at Butler or say anything to him on her way out. The door was closed behind them, leaving Harper and Butler alone.

Harper picked a pencil off his desk and began playing with it. "Have trouble on the mission, Butler?"

"Not particularly."

"It's most unusual to get requests such as Ms. Willoughby

just made. Evidently she didn't like you very much."

"Evidently."

"You didn't try anything with her, did you?"

"Like what?"

Harper smiled and shrugged. "You know."

"I don't know."

"Well, you have a certain reputation in the Institute, Butler. You're always trying to seduce the ladies."

"I think I should be judged on the results of my missions, not on nasty, unfounded rumors."

"I'm not so sure they're so unfounded. Ms. Willoughby seems most hostile to you, and there must be a reason."

"You should have asked her why."

"I'm sure she'd be too much of a lady to denounce you for trying to seduce her on an important mission like this one."

"I don't think you should let your erotic imagination run away with you."

Harper shuffled some papers on his desk. "Well, I guess that will be all, Butler. Have a nice trip back, and my congratulations once again."

"Thank you, sir."

They shook hands, then Butler turned and left the office.

BUTLER

SMART BOMBS

is the second in the
exciting new series from Leisure Books
featuring the renegade superspy!
Other BUTLER titles include:

#1   The Hydra Conspiracy

Follow Butler's next adventure in

THE SLAYBOYS

coming in October from Leisure Books.